Holidays
with the HORDE

WHEELS & HOGS

BOOK FOUR

by
D.M. EARL

Cover designed by Margreet Asselbergs

Rebel Edit & Design

http://www.rebeleditdesign.com/

Wheels & Hogs Series

This series is a continuation from each of the prior books. There will not be major cliffhangers at the end of each book, there might be parts of each story that are either unresolved or unanswered, so please be aware of this.

It is suggested that you follow the order of the series and read each book in their specific order.

********Cautions/Warning********

Mature Audience 18+

Contains Adult Language & Sexual Situations

COPYRIGHT

Acknowledgements

When writing a book, there are so many people involved in the story. I try to make sure and mention everyone but please do not be offended if I miss someone.

To my Beta's who at the drop of a hat make the time to not only read, but also actually make sure the storyline is consistent throughout. Also they take into account the different POV's and make sure they aren't changing from chapter to chapter. So a huge shout-out to Karen (Kaz), Sam, Laura and Shanean. Without you ladies I would never get my WIP to the editor.

My PA's Laura & Shanean who are there for me day after day. You both keep me sane. Your help and assistance with all the social media allows me to dedicate more time to my writing. Thank you both so very much.

To my ladies in D.M.'s Horde you all have become very special to me. It started with the reader's group but has grown into something so much more. You are my book family. Every day I speak to one or more of you. Your post, emails, cards and notes mean the world to me. Know Ya'll have a special place in my heart.

Bloggers hell without each and every one of you I would still be trying to figure this out. I sincerely thank you for all you do because of your love of reading. I am forever in your debt.

Love between the Sheets thank you for always making time to do my cover reveals and release dates. You ladies are so professional and never have I had any issues. You make that part of my writing so easy and for that I am grateful.

Margreet Asselbergs you are the shining star in my writing career. I am blessed to have found you as a graphic designer who creates everything exactly how I want it even though I can't explain it to you. You get in my head and just frigging amaze me. Besides your mad skills I am proud to call you a friend. I can go to you anytime and you always pull me back and for that I have no words.

Dana Hook for being the best editor out there. You never say no even when you should probably and for that I love you. Your dedication to what you do is phenomenal and your skills are outstanding. Being able to call you my friend is one of the greatest gifts I've received since I started writing.

Chris & Katie thank you for giving my words the final once over to make sure everything is how it should be. Your patience and dedication to this part of a book is what makes the end product that much better.

Readers I am simply amazed that Ya'll not only purchase my books but also read them, review them and seem to love them. I have no words to explain how much this truly means to me. Because of each of you I am on the road to living my dream by telling stories. And know each story has a special place in my heart as each and every one of you do.

Chuck you are my love, have made life simply wonderful. Your support, love and understanding make this journey so special. Knowing you have my back no matter if I succeed or fail allows me to pursue this dream. For that I have no words to let you know how much that means. All I can say is I love you heart and soul.

Table of Contents

Dedication

I dedicate this book to every person who at some point in their lives have struggled with the word *'family'*. This word can mean so many different things for each of us. As you delve into Holidays with the Horde, really see that the meaning of *'family'* is generally the same no matter who you are. People, who love and support each other no matter what. You don't have to be blood related.

Believe me I know, as some of the people closest to me are people I have met through the years who I hold close to my heart. I don't see them all the time and we are now all over, but I hope they know that no matter what I will always consider them family.

So to all my extended family whether you live in Piper City, Lemont, Oak Forest, Romeoville, Burbank or where ever I cherish each and every memory we have created and can't wait to make more.

Ya'll are my family and I love each and every one of you.

Chapter 1

Gabriel

"Furn! Come on, wake up, Furn. We have to trow the turkury in the oven for Tanksgiving. Everyone is coming today, even Gramma, so we have to get ready. Come on, Furn. Pease?"

I hear the sweet little voice close to my ear, just as Fern starts to wake up. Chuckling, I pull Fern close, whispering, "Sugar, you better get moving before Emma decides to 'trow the turkury' in all by herself."

Pulling away from me, Fern opens her eyes, and Emma's face lights up before she squeals.

"Furn, you're awake. Let's go. We have work to do."

She flies off the bed like a little hurricane and leaves our room. Thinking of her biological mother, Lydia, I silently thank her for the gift she left behind for us.

Throwing the blankets off, Fern grabs her robe and turns to me.

"Do you want me to start the coffee...oh, and can you see if Charlie's up yet?"

"Sugar, for you I'll do anything. I'll get the coffee while you take care of the little princess. She's so excited about the holidays. They both deserve it. It's been hell for both of them since losing Lydia, so we have to make the holidays special for them this year. Ann should be here shortly, I suspect." Ann's their grandma, whom we share the kids with.

Fern enters the bathroom, and I reflect on all that has happened recently. First and foremost, my Fern is in remission, and I thank God everyday for that. I couldn't have handled anything happening to her. But we lost Lydia, Fern's childhood friend, who was in the hospital at the same time as her, also fighting cancer. That's how we came to have both Emma and Charlie with us. Lydia knew her mom, Ann, wasn't going to be able to handle the kids alone, being diabetic. So, Lydia left details on how she wanted the kids raised, choosing us, along with Ann, to raise her children. That's how we've come to be here today, and we have a lot to be thankful for. The Horde and friends are coming to our house for Thanksgiving dinner, and Fern's been busting her ass to make it perfect.

Hearing her opening the bathroom door, I sit up and wait on the side of the bed. She comes to stand between my legs, putting her hands on my shoulders. She takes my breath away, just as she always has.

"Gabriel, before we get started and the day runs away from us, I wanted to take a minute to let you know what I'm thankful for."

She leans down and brings her forehead to touch mine, bringing us eye to eye. I watch the color in her hazel eyes as they sparkle with happiness.

"You, Gabriel. That's what I'm thankful for. You make my life complete, and give me everything I will ever need—your support, devotion, and your love. You've pulled me through cancer, and I have no words that will ever let you know how much you mean to me. I love you, honey."

She leans back and softly touches her lips to mine in one of the sweetest kisses, putting all her love and emotion behind it. After a bit, she stands up and squeezes my shoulders. I watch my wife walk out of our room, knowing that there is nothing out

there better than what we have. It means everything to me, and I
intend to treasure it every single day.

Sitting in our family room with Charlie watching football,
I'm amazed at the fantastic smells coming from the kitchen.
Fern, Ann, Emma, and Archie are all in there, doing whatever it
is they do to create an unbelievable Thanksgiving dinner.
They've been at it for hours. I was a bit shocked when I opened
the door to see both Ann and Archie here so early. Ann I
expected, but not Archie. She doesn't come across as the typical
female because she's such a hard-ass, but she has a heart of gold.
Never one to hang with the women, she's always been more
comfortable hanging with us guys, drinking beer and watching
sports, but since Ann's started coming around, Archie's
changed...or maybe she's becoming the woman she's wanting to
be.

When Ann moved into the cabin behind Wheels & Hogs
with the kids, it became apparent that it was a struggle for her to
take care of herself and them alone. After Lydia passed away,
and I was dealing with Fern's illness, Archie and Willow gave up
their apartment in town and moved into the cabin with Ann.
They've created their own little family, both women seemingly
love being around Ann. For Ann, it filled the void of losing her
only daughter. She's taken both Archie and Willow under her
wing, and Emma and Charlie adore them.

Charlie's dozing off in my lap when the doorbell rings. He's
immediately up and alert, jumping off me and screaming wildly.

"Is it Cadence? Come on, let's open the door! It might be
Cadence."

His excitement's contagious as we go to the door. Looking through the glass, I see Bear, Ugly, and Stash. Knowing Charlie isn't going to be happy it isn't his buddy, I lean down and whisper in his ear.

"Charlie, it's the biker dudes. Remember you wanted them to come? You invited them, so let's show them a good time. What do you say, kiddo?"

He grins wildly and swings his arms around. "Yay, the bikers are here. Let them in so we can play Legos."

Opening the door, I'm shocked to see Ugly with a bouquet of flowers, Bear holding a bottle of wine, and Stash carrying some kind of baked goods. Holy shit! They clean up good. Knowing they went Nomad from the MC club they were involved in out West before Fern's charity ride, and were actually making Tranquility their home, simply amazed me. They look the part of members of a badass club, but deep down, they're some of the nicest guys you could ever meet.

Before I can say anything, Charlie grabs Bear's free hand and pulls him in.

"Happy Thanksgiving, Bear. Let's play Legos." Laughing, Bear follows him in.

"Hey, Charlie. Let me give these to Fern first, and then we can grab the Legos. I've got something out in the bike for you too."

Charlie gets excited as the men come in, dropping their gifts into Fern's arms. She loves these guys, and it shows in the greeting they receive after she passes the gifts to Archie. They each get a hug and a kiss on the cheek. She has always been the maternal one who makes everyone welcome.

I see the look Ugly has on his face when he realizes Archie's here. When he turns away from her, I see it written all over his face—he wants Archie. I'll have to speak to Fern about this, 'cause I'm not sure they would be a good fit for each other, and Fern will make sure no one ends up hurt.

The doorbell rings again, and Charlie comes running to greet the newcomers. Des and Dee Dee, along with her kids, Jagger and Daisy, stand in the front. The Powers family, Cadence, Trinity, along with baby Hope is standing right behind them. I open the door wide, letting everyone in, and notice how unhappy Daisy seems.

As everyone greets each other, Des and Cadence drop off their handfuls of food before making their way back outside to get whatever else is left in their cars. Once they return, I step back to take in the people Fern and I consider family, but a familiar face is missing. I look around and find Daisy sitting in the far corner of the family room on the floor, and for the first time, I notice how gaunt she looks. She looks like she's lost quite a bit of weight since I saw her last, and it's weight she couldn't't afford to lose. Her eyes have black circles under them, but what stands out the most is that she's alienating herself from her family. Something serious is going on with her, so I make a mental note to have a word with Des.

Chapter 2

Fern

Thanksgiving Dinner

As I watch Gabriel try to get everyone settled at the tables, I sit with the ladies, trying to get all the food together so we can serve it up hot. I'm so happy my heart could burst. Having everyone here has made my dreams of a true family holiday come true. Over the last year, they've come to mean so much to both Gabriel and I. When I was sick, each and every one of them stepped up to help us. I will never forget that, ever.

Opening the oven, I pull out the mashed potatoes first, then the sweet potato casserole. "Willow, can you butter up the mashed potatoes and put them on the counter please? Archie, can you grab the casserole and place that also on the counter?"

Cadence comes in and slams the back door behind him. "Hey, Mom. The turkey's done on the grill. Should I bring it in now? Before I can answer, the door bangs shut again.

"Fern, the deep fried turkey's done. Do you want us to bring it in? I'll need something to put it on."

Smiling at Axe, I go to grab a serving tray for him and one for Cadence. The men have some sort of contest going on about which turkey will taste the best. I'm guessing both will be good, but the one I'm making in the oven with stuffing has always been Gabriel's favorite. Thank God when they re-did our home, they put in the double stove, along with an additional smaller oven by the island. It makes big dinners like this a lot easier on me.

"Here you both go. Bring them in and put them on the far counter. We can let them cool a bit before Des and Gabriel carve them up. Sound good?" Both nod as they head back outside.

I can't hold back my smile as I look at the three tables, all beautiful, with flowers in the center. The kids tried to use the same plates for each table, and for Ann, we used Lydia's dishes. I miss my friend everyday, but having Charlie and Emma with us makes it a bit easier. We still have her with us through them.

As we continue to get the rest of the food heated up, along with the cold items out on the counters, I notice Dee Dee looking at Daisy in the corner. Glancing between my best friend and her daughter, I'm taken aback at how the young girl seems so distant and detached from the rest of us. Finally, Dee Dee approaches her, squatting down so they're at eye level. Dee Dee says something to her, and when she gets no reply, she grabs the ear buds out of Daisy's ears.

"What the hell, Mom? Why'd you do that? I was listening to that song. "

Everyone goes quiet. Daisy is usually such a quiet and happy girl, and never back talks her mom.

"Fern, can we use your room for a minute?"

Nodding, I watch Dee Dee, Daisy, and Des, head towards our room. Looking around, I catch Gabriel's eyes and he shrugs. Neither of us have any idea what's going on. Turning around, I see Jagger nervously looking down the hall where his family just went. I give Gabriel a nod towards Jagger, and as I go to check the dinner rolls, I see my husband putting his hand on Jagger's shoulder, directing him away from the others.

Looking over at my husband, working his magic and taking Jagger's mind off what's going on, I get back to what I'm doing. The moment I start, I feel a sharp pain in my wrist, causing me to drop the tray of dinner rolls. Gabriel's there in an instant, grabbing my hand and looking over the red welt. Moving me to the sink, he turns on the cold water and gently places my wrist under the flow.

"Don't look too bad, but it'll sting for a bit."

Smiling to myself, I feel his eyes on me. Looking up, I can't stop myself from giggling. "Something funny, Sugar? You think I'm being too overprotective, right? Is that what you're thinking in that beautiful head of yours?"

"Gabriel, don't worry so much. It's just a small burn. Everything's fine…well, almost everything. Do you have any clue as to what's going on with Daisy? Has Des said anything to you, because Dee Dee hasn't mentioned anything to me?"

He goes to speak, just as the doorbell rings. Seems like the rest of our family has arrived, and just in time.

I wipe my hands on the dishtowel and head towards the door, where I find Cadence's mom and brothers. Greeting them warmly as they walk in, Cadence's mom, Carol, kisses my cheek.

"Fern, I'm going to drop this off in the kitchen. Griffin, give Fern those bottles of wine and go get the rest of the stuff out of the car. Ryker, hand those flowers off to Archie and help your brother."

I was so happy when Carol and her boys decided to stay in Tranquility. I know it means a lot to Cadence, and to the rest of us. She's become a dear friend to our little group, especially Gabriel and I. This holiday could not be any better.

As we all find a seat, I run back and forth, making sure the food is hot and everyone has what they need. Waiting until they're all settled, I clear my throat to get their attention.

"I don't want to get all mushy, especially with so many alpha men in the room, but I wanted to say a quick and sincere thank you to all of you for everything you've done for us. I'm forever grateful to have you all in our lives. We've been so very blessed, and I needed to share that. Gabriel and I would have never gotten through this past year without you. So, with that, let's eat!"

"Furn, can I say Grace? Momma always said it before we ate." Emma's small, adorable voice asks.

My heart clenches as I glance at Ann, whose eyes are shiny with tears, then to Gabriel, who only stares back at me. We're spiritual people, but never really worried about saying Grace, yet, since the kids have started staying here, we have incorporated it into our dinner routine. I can't believe I forgot that today, of all days.

I look at Lydia's daughter, who wants to include her momma in our Thanksgiving dinner. My heart is truly full, and once again, I'm reminded of how much I miss my friend.

"Please, Emma, go ahead. Everyone, grab a hand and let's say Grace so we can eat this amazing looking meal."

As Emma says the prayer, I look around the table and see my family, none of who is blood related, as they bow their heads. Women, men, bikers, and kids, all sharing my favorite holiday together. There's no place else I would rather be than right here, in this moment.

Chapter 3

Gabriel

"Sugar, what's weighing on your mind? Everything was phenomenal today. You had the house looking great, the food was fantastic, and everyone seemed to have a great time.

"I know, Gabriel, but I'm worried about Daisy. Were you able to find out anything when you spoke to Jagger? Does he know what's going on?"

"No, Sugar. When we talked, he was as confused as we are. He told me that for some reason, Daisy's been distant with him, and he has no clue as to why. He's genuinely upset because they've always been so close. I'm not sure what we can do, but I'm gonna try to have a word with Des, and when you feel it's right, you should do the same with Dee Dee."

"Daisy came to me and apologized. She seemed genuinely sorry, but I'm not sure if it was her idea or Dee Dee's."

"Well, it's nothing we can fix, especially not tonight, so let's relax and think about what a great day we had." Lying behind her, I rub my hands across her stomach, then slowly move up, brushing the fullness of her breasts before coming to her shoulders. I start to massage them, trying to release her tension. Hearing her sigh, I feel her body begin to relax, and it brings a smile to my face. I thrust my hips closer to her ass, showing her how she affects me. She pushes back against my hard length, and I groan. Damn, this woman gets to me every time.

"Gabriel..."

With Emma and Charlie spending the night at Ann's, we have the place to ourselves. The house without the kids is rare these days, and I for one, want to take advantage of it.

Moving my hands down, I concentrate on the swell of her breasts. I massage them from underneath, making sure I concentrate on her nipples, bringing the blood to the surface. She loves it when I play with her breasts, especially her nipples, and her moans turn me on even more. I can feel the blood moving to the center of my body, specifically to my cock.

"Arms up. I need to get this shirt off of you."

Lifting her arms, I remove her camisole, and instantly place my hands on her naked tits. God, I love how full they are, and how they fit my hands perfectly. Her rosy nipples are hard, and I continue to play with them—pinching and pulling until she grabs my hands with hers to add more pressure. My Fern is turned on, and it's a sight to see.

"Gabriel, please…please… "

"Please what, Sugar? Tell me what you want. Need your words, Fern."

"I need you to…oh God! I need to feel you inside of me."

I take my time teasing her, making sure she's good and ready for me. Since her chemo treatments, I've had to get inventive with getting her ready for me. Reaching down, I remove her PJ bottoms, along with her panties, before I do the same with mine. My hard length bounces towards Fern, knowing where it wants to be. I reach around her hip to place my fingers on her center. I feel her moisture coat my fingers, letting me know she's enjoying this as much as I am. I push down on her swollen clit and rub it in circles. Her hips start to jerk up and down, trying to find a rhythm that will hit her exactly where she needs it. She's panting as her hands grasp the sheets in front of her tightly.

"Sugar, hands on the headboard, and don't let go, no matter what."

Raising myself over her and rolling her to her back, I gently spread her legs with mine and settle between them. My hand goes between our bodies and once again, I can feel her excitement by the wetness greeting my fingers. I slowly enter her tight cunt. She moves up and down as I continue with my forward push. She loves foreplay, so I give her what she likes, taking time to touch and feel her, brushing over each and every part of her body. I reach down to suck on her nipple, giving it the attention it needs before moving to the other one. Her body trembles with excitement, but her hands stay wrapped around the headboard, her knuckles white from the effort.

Her cunt tightens around my fingers, and I know she's close. I move my fingers, putting pressure on the rough bundle of nerves deep inside. It causes her back to arch as she screams my name with her release."

Almost losing it myself, I work her until she starts to come down. I gently remove my fingers and bring them to my mouth as Fern watches me lick them clean. Her eyes darken. Not able to wait another moment, I plunge into her warmth, the sensation so intense, and my entire body shakes. I start off slow, but build to a tempo we both know very well. I sense it when she's getting close again, so I increase the speed of my hips, wanting both of us to finish at the same time. With her hands still holding the headboard tight, all she has to use are her legs, which she tightly wraps around my hips, her bare feet pressing into my ass each time I thrust inside of her. The familiar pressure in my lower back starts, and my balls tighten. Knowing I can't hold off any longer, I place a finger on Fern's clit and start to tap it firmly. Her breath quickens as her hips start to rock with mine. I can feel the sweat rolling down my neck as I continue to push in and out of her warmth, her juices making my actions smooth and easy. Knowing that I'm seconds away, I lean in and bite the skin between her shoulder and neck, then whisper in her ear.

"Let go for me, Sugar. I wanna feel your pussy tighten around my cock as I cum."

Her legs tighten around me as she once again arches her back. I take her hardened nipple into my mouth—pulling, stretching it out, and biting down on it. She screams when I start to feel the pull. Suddenly, my vision goes black and I let out a growl as stream after stream of my cum fills her. She spasms as her walls tighten, making my orgasm longer, until she drains me completely.

Once we both catch our breath, I gently pull out as she moans, letting me know she doesn't want me to leave. Pulling her to me, I grab the covers and throw them over us, and then I wrap my front around her back, my knees bent, as her legs move to allow mine to twine with hers.

"Sugar, you are my treasure. I love you so much."

She snuggles closer, and I feel her body relax as she starts to fade off to sleep.

"I love you more. You're my life."

Chapter 4

Des

Sitting in my office, I'm once again taken aback at Daisy's behavior. First the scene at Thanksgiving, and now last night. The argument between Dee Dee and Daisy was horrible, and the nasty things Daisy spewed toward her mother stunned me. I had to bite my fucking tongue, but in the end, I couldn't let it go on, and added my two cents, to Dee Dee's dismay.

Now I'm in the doghouse, and neither female in my house is talking to each other, or me. Even Jagger's keeping his distance from his sister. Speaking of Jagger, I need to talk to him today, because I noticed the box of condoms I gave him is empty. I wanted him to be safe, and apparently he is, but thinking back now, I should have spoken to Dee Dee before I made the decision to give them to him. Shit's gonna hit the fan, I'm sure.

My mind goes back to Thanksgiving, and Daisy's attitude in general. I was knocked on my ass over her attitude towards her mom 'cause she's always such a good kid. I understand being fourteen, and I sort of understand the whole "hormones" issues with women, but the mouth and language on that girl, I don't get. Both Dee Dee and I tried to speak to her at Doc's on Thanksgiving, and later when we got home. Nothing we said was getting through to her, and she acted like we were ganging up on her. It pissed Dee off, and that started World War III. Damn, those women can scream, yell, and then scream more.

A knock on the door interrupts my thoughts. "Come in." Looking up, I watch Cadence walk in and take a seat in one of the chairs.

"What the fuck is up with Daisy? Trinity 'bout lost her mind with the way she talked to Dee Dee, and her attitude through the rest of the day. Come on, let me have it. Is it a boy, bad grades? What could a teenage girl who's always so happy and sweet be so upset about?"

"No fucking idea, Cadence. She won't talk to either one of us. All I know is Daisy is in shutdown mode. She's not speaking to Dee, Jagger, or me. I do my best to keep the kids happy, giving them whatever they need and want, even when Dee Dee says no. Dee Dee gets mad at me, but I'm always able to convince her to my way of thinking, if you know what I mean." I wink at Cadence and laugh.

"Okay, old man. Don't need to know about that shit. Don't gross me out with thoughts of your old ass doing the nasty. That's a visual I *don't* need."

As we continue to banter back and forth, I pull up my emails to see if anything important has come in. Seeing one from Dee Dee, I open it and just about fall out of my chair. Cadence immediately sits up straight, trying to glance at the screen. I move quickly to close the window, but he's quick .

"Jesus Christ! Y'all are sexting each other? Really Des that is fuckin' gross dude. Shit, I won't be able to look at Dee Dee again without that shit in my head. Grow up, old man. Both of you are too old for that. Shouldn't you be like, sitting in a rocking chair, eating Fig Newton's?" He holds his gut and laughs.

I get up and move around the desk, ready to knock him upside the head, but before I can, he leans away from me.

"Listen hear, ya punk. I'll knock you on your ass any day of the week. Forget what you saw. Why are you even here?"

He looks at me, and I swear I see a flash of fear is in his eyes, but it disappears quickly.

"I need your help…well, I need all of the Horde's help. I want to surprise Trinity and get married on New Year's Eve, but it has to be without her help. This pregnancy is killing her, and I don't want her any more upset than she already is. What d'ya think? Can we pull this off? She deserves the best of the best, and that's what I plan to give her. Been savin', and I talked to the priest." I give him a curious look. "Yeah, you son of a bitch. I did it, so I just need to get everything else in order. I'm thinking small for this one, and we can have a huge party once this baby comes. Trinity is feeling really bad that she has one child and is expecting another, and we aren't married yet. Was thinking of doing it here at Wheels & Hogs. What d'ya say?"

"You're going from one of the best mechanics in Tranquility to the new wedding planner? Damn, boy. The women are gonna love you, but Trinity might not find it funny."

His face turns a bright shade of red, and before he can even spit out one word, I bust out laughing. When he realizes I'm only messing with him, he joins in on the laughter, and this is what Wolf walks into.

"What's so funny, and why am I always left out? Come on, you can tell me."

Glancing at Cadence, then Wolf, I decide to have some fun with this. They're always ganging up on me and giving me shit, so payback's a bitch.

"Well, Wolf, it looks like Cadence is changing professions. He just informed me that he's gonna be a wedding planner, and he's starting with his own. He needs our help to plan his wedding to Trinity, and he's picked New Year's Eve for the date. So can you get your iPad and start taking some notes on what he wants, his…what do they call that shit? Yeah, his wedding color scheme. Oh, and maybe we can go cake tasting together one night."

Cadence jumps up and pushes me back. I fly backwards towards my desk, slamming my ass directly on top of it. Damn, this boy's been working out. Laughing so hard my gut hurts, Wolf joins me. Shit, it feels good to mess with my boys. Knowing how much this means to Cadence, of course we'll all be on board, but that doesn't mean we're not gonna be smartasses along the way.

Chapter 5

Dee Dee

Hearing Des' laugh, I walk down the hall to his office. His laugh always sends shivers down my spine. That man, no matter what he does, turns me on. From working on a car or bike, to cleaning house, or mowing the grass, I'm in a constant state of being turned on. *Damn him*, I think, smiling to myself. Not something to really complain about.

Opening the door, I immediately see Wolf, Cadence, and my man, perched around his desk, looking at the papers spread out across Des' desk. As I approach, they're so absorbed in what they're doing, that they don't hear me until I say, "What are you boys up to?"

They all jump, Cadence more than the rest. I immediately feel bad because knowing his history he likely sunk back into his hell momentarily. Reaching out, I rub my hand up and down his back.

"Sorry, honey. I didn't mean to startle you. Thought you guys heard me come in and close the door. So, what are you planning? Looks to be something big. Need some help?"

Turning to me with a shit-eating grin, Cadence nods his head. Pushing the papers my way, he waits for me to read them. My eyes get bigger and bigger as I realize what it is I'm reading. Holy crap, he's gonna do it. Looking back up at him, I smile and give him a huge hug.

"Whatever I can do, just let me know, Cadence. Is it a surprise, or is Trinity in on it? I know she hasn't been feeling good, morning sickness and all. Poor girl."

"Nope. I'd really like to surprise her. Not sure everyone will be able to keep their mouths shut, but we'll deal with it when it happens. I have no idea where to even start, Dee Dee. Do you have time right now to go over this stuff with me? If not, I can stop by your house later tonight. I don't want Trin to get curious and start asking questions. I was gonna talk to Archie and Willow to see if they would help too. I want Trinity's day to be the best day ever, 'cause she deserves it, so I don't wanna put any restrictions on anything. Not that I won the lottery or anything, but I've been saving, so I can give you my budget. After that, don't care if you ladies blow the whole amount. How does that sound?"

"Awesome, honey, but be careful telling the girls that. Could be dangerous. Where were you thinking of having this wedding? At a venue, a hall, or here at Wheels & Hogs? I can work with whatever you want. I've thrown quite a few parties in my day."

Cadence gives Des a worried look before he looks back to me.

"I was thinking about having it here at Wheels & Hogs. This place holds a special place in our hearts. Not to mention, we live right upstairs."

Watching his face, looking worried and concerned, I smile and wrap my arms around his waist.

"That would be perfect. I know how much this place means to you especially. We'll have our hands full, trying to make sure it's clean and ready for such a special event, but we'll get it done. It will be perfect."

Hearing Wolf clear his throat, we all turn.

"Cadence, brother, I want to put this out there. It's up to you, obviously, but it will be hard to surprise Trinity if she's home, and seeing everything being delivered. Why don't you and Trinity get married at my house? We can really do up the pole barn and gazebo to make it a beautiful venue. How does that sound?"

"Shit. I never thought about that, Wolf. You wouldn't mind all that shit at your house? I think it would work better at your place to make it a real surprise, especially in such a beautiful place. Thank you, brother. It means the world."

Des

Watching Dee Dee, Cadence, and even Wolf, begin to plan an impromptu wedding, I realize Dee Dee didn't tell me why she stopped in. It made me nervous not knowing, but I didn't want to pursue it. Whatever it is, I'm sure I'm still in the doghouse. I know she has a lot of shit weighing on her mind, and eventually, she's gonna unload it all on me, so I better be prepared.

Chapter 6

Daisy

I'm still feeling bad about how things went down on Thanksgiving at Doc and Fern's. I've been trying to make a thank you card for them, but I keep getting distracted by the noises coming out of Jagger's room. I hate that she's in my home. I hate her and her friends so much. My brother has no clue that he's dating the devil's daughter.

Walking to the kitchen to get a drink, I hear someone come up behind me. Before I can turn around to see who it is, I feel her wrap her one hand around my arm holding me in place as her fingers pinch the back of my arm. It's still bruised from the last time her and her friends pinched the shit out of me. The pinching, pushing into lockers, pulling my hair while sitting behind me in class, knocking my books out of my hand then pushing me when I am picking them up, making funny of me on social media and just being so mean even though I have tried to avoid all of them is really getting old. Between the pinching, pushing into lockers, pulling my hair while sitting behind me in class, knocking my books out of my hand then pushing me when I am picking them up and just being so mean even though I have tried to avoid all of them.

"What are you doing, you little bitch? Spying on me again? That's really sick. Wait until I tell the other girls, they won't be happy."

Turning around, I look into the hateful face of Sabrina, better known as Brina to her friends. Brina and her mean girl clique have made my first year of high school a living hell. And to make matters worse, she's dating my brother, which means I have to see her, not only at school, but at home as well. I'm ready to pull my hair out, at least before they do.

"I had no idea you were even here, and if I did, spying on you is gross. Especially when you are visiting with my brother. I'm not some sicko. I'm in here to get a drink, that's all."

Trying to move past her, she gets really close before pushing me back into the refrigerator, hard enough for me to yelp. I hear Jagger call from his room.

"Daisy? You okay? You're clumsy ass didn't't trip again, did you?"

Sabrina looks down the hall, then back at me, with a vicious look on her face.

"Yeah, Jagger, she fell." I hear his laughter, believing every word. "She'll probably have a few bruises...it was a mighty hard fall."

She shoves me again, this time harder. I was a little more prepared this time and braced myself, making it hurt more. She grabs me by the arm and throws me across the room, causing me to lose my footing, and I slam into the ceramic tile floor, just as Jagger enters the room.

Looking up at my brother as he reaches down to help me up, I'm not sure how much he's seen, that is until he glares over at Sabrina.

"Get your shit and get gone. What the hell do you think you're doing, pushing Daisy around like that? She's my sister. No one, and I mean no one hurts her."

"Jagger, honey, I didn't mean any harm. You know me, I wouldn't do anything to hurt Daisy. Right, Daisy? Go on, tell him."

Listening to her pathetic whining, I really am tempted to tell my brother all the hell her and her friends put me through, but that would only make things even worse for me, so I lie. I don't need any more attention from these girls than I already have.

"Jagger, don't be mad at her. Sabrina was just helping me, and when I got up, I lost my balance. What you saw wasn't her pushing me, she was trying to catch my arm and prevent me from face planting. That's all."

I start to panic as I watch him thinking my excuse over. I need him to believe me. I see how she and her clique pick on other girls at school, and I want to try and stay on her good side, if she even has one. Finally, Jagger relaxes, seeming to believe me.

"You gonna be okay? Should I call Mom or Des?"

At this, Sabrina smirks, but because she's standing behind Jagger, he doesn't see it.

"No, I'm good. Why don't you two get some snacks or something. I'm just gonna go back to my room and chill. Thanks again, Sabrina. I appreciate your help."

Her voice is smooth as honey. "No problem, Daisy…not a problem at all. I hope you feel better. See you at school."

I walk away, feeling like I dodged a bullet, for now.

Waking up to Mom and Des coming home, I know it's only a matter of time before they come to give me the third degree because of my attitude. They have every right in the world to question and punish me, so I'm not complaining. I can never tell them what's going on at school, and now at home. I can't tell them about the hell I've been living through, each and every day, because if they know I'm being bullied, the shit would hit the fan. If the girls are this bad, I don't want to imagine how much worse they could make my life, so mums the word. Maybe they will get tired of this game and eventually leave me alone. I can only hope.

Chapter 7

Wolf

Sitting in my family room, looking at the small Christmas tree I cut down earlier, I come to the decision that it's a pretty nice tree. Not too big, not too small, and with the lights and ornaments, it looks just right. I wouldn't't have gone through the trouble, but this is where everyone will be for Christmas Eve. The tree is for the kiddos, to put them in the Christmas spirit.

Thinking about the kids coming brings a smile to my face. Hope's crawling, and so close now to walking. She's got the best of both her parents in her. Emma and Charlie are coming out of their shells, and we're all finally getting to see their little personalities, and they're getting big. Then there's Daisy and Jagger. It's so hard to believe that they're teenagers, but that's exactly what they are now.

I know that everyone's worried about Daisy, and so am I. I've been keeping an eye on her, and I know that whatever it is that's bothering her, it has to be something going on at school. It seems to have started when Jagger started bringing a girl around. I asked Jagger about her when he was at the shop, and he said her name was Sabrina. He also informed me she was just someone he was hanging with, which I think is safe to assume, he's having sex with.

The doorbell ringing brings me out of my musings. Going to the door, I look through the upper glass to see my brother glaring back at me. Damn it, now what? Opening the door and moving to let him in, Axe stomps into the house, and I can feel the anger bouncing off of him.

"What the fuck, Wolf? For years I have begged you to have Christmas here for our family, or what's left of it, and you've always said no. Des asks, and immediately Christmas Eve is at Wolf's. Explain this shit to me, asshole."

"Axe, I don't have to explain shit to you, brother. For the last...what, ten plus years? These people have been my family. They've been there for the good and the bad, so yeah, Des asked and I said yes. He and Dee Dee are having issues with Daisy. Cadence is trying to plan a surprise wedding for Trinity, which is gonna be here also. She's having a hard time with this pregnancy, and Cadence wants to give her the best of everything, including a surprise wedding. So, for Christmas Eve, if you want to bring someone, or tell Momma and the family to come, I'm good with that. But you know that Momma is going to call all of them, and I can't help the way I feel. It will never change, Axe, no matter what you say. There are people in our family that are damaged, and I've chosen to not have anything to do with them."

I want to explain to my brother why our biological family is no longer a part of my life, but the doorbell rings again. I don't need to answer it since Cadence walks right on in with a smile on his face.

"Hey, Wolf. It's not a bad time is it? Want to get an idea of where we would have the wedding, then dinner, so I can give the girls the list of what we need. Hey, Axe. How ya doin'?"

"Of course Wolf has time for you, brother. It's his blood brother he never can find time for. Fuck this, I'm out. Don't wanna spoil your fun, Wolf. I get it now. Fuck the rest of us, right?"

With that, he walks past a shocked Cadence, whose mouth is hanging open as Axe slams the door shut.

40

"Jesus, dude. Didn't mean to piss him off. What the fuck was he going on about? Shit, never mind. I'll come back later."

"Cadence, no worries. Really. This is what happens between Axe and me, and has been for years. I know in the last couple years, we've gotten closer, but there are things about me you don't know. One day—not today—but one day, I will share them with you. So for now, let's get to the important stuff. Why are you here again?"

Cadence and I spend a few hours going around the house, gazebo, and pole barn, to see what would work for his upcoming nuptials. He stays long enough to have a beer before he heads back to Trinity and Hope.

So, once again, I'm sitting here looking at my tree, when the doorbell rings, *again*. Getting up, I answer the door, finding Dee Dee, Archie, and Willow, with bags and boxes in their arms.

"We're here to decorate your man cave for our holiday dinner." Dee Dee announces, trying to get past me to put down her bags, the other women on her heels.

"Is that it?"

"Not even close. Remember, the wedding is going to be here, so we have Christmas decorations and stuff for the wedding also. The rest is in my SUV."

Walking out of my house filled with women taking it over, I think back to a time when I had no one in my life. Though Axe can be an ass, maybe it's finally time to cross that bridge and deal with the shit that is my family.

Watching Dee Dee, Archie, and Willow go through their bags, putting up decorations around my house, I feel a warmth in my home that's been missing, and that's the laughter and touch of a woman. Glancing up, I see Willow watching me.

When our eyes meet, she starts to blush, which is cute as hell. She's a knockout, and I know she has a crush on me. I've known it for years, though I never thought to go there because of our friendship, and there's a lot about me she doesn't know. Not to mention our connection with the Horde.

I don't want to lose the friendship we have, but it could be worth it. I mean, Willow is beautiful, smart, shy, funny, and she's loyal to those she loves.

Looking at her from the corner of my eye, I see she's still looking at me, so I look back. I look her up and down, then back to her face. Her face is flushed, and I'm not sure if it's from embarrassment or excitement. But seeing her nipples poking through her shirt, I'm assuming it's from excitement. I give her a sexy smile, and she returns it with her own. Damn, I didn't know she had it in her. Maybe I misjudged her, and she's not as innocent as I thought.

Well, maybe it's time to see if this crush of hers is worth pursuing. From the hardness in my jeans, I know she's getting to me too. Maybe we should see where it could go, but that's only if she can accept all of me.

Chapter 8

Jagger

"Damn, don't stop, Sabrina...fuck! That feels so good, baby."

I watch as her mouth goes up and down my cock. This girl can give head like no other. Not that I've had that much experience, but damn! Her mouth is amazing. Sabrina pops my cock out of her mouth to lick the head like an ice cream cone, concentrating on the slit in the middle. I can feel the tingle start, and I know I'm not gonna last long if she keeps this up. Trying to grab her, she evades me, and rams my cock to the back of her throat, then moans. The vibration does me in, and I blow my load down her willing throat. I'm so immersed in it, that I don't hear my bedroom door open, but I do hear a gasp.

"What in the hell is going on in here? Holy shit! I mean, I don't know what I mean. Get off the floor, Sabrina, and please, son, cover up. I can't believe this. We trusted you after school to be home alone with your sister. I've told you time and time again, no visitors, and definitely none of this, whatever this is."

"It's called a blow job, Mrs. Davis. I'm sure you know what that is, or don't you?"

I can't believe she just said that to my mom. Shit.

"Sabrina, get your sh...stuff together, and get out of here. I need to talk to my mom. Go, get out. I'll talk to you later."

She grabs her stuff and comes up to me, lifting up on her toes as she presses her lips to mine. I know her intent, and I don't play along. Putting my hands on her shoulders, I push her away. She looks pissed, but I just don't care. I wanted her out, right now. She shouldn't have disrespected my mom.

She goes to pass my mom on her way out, staring at her intently as she uses her fingers to wipe at the corners of her mouth. I can literally see the steam coming from my mom's ears, but she doesn't say a word.

"Mom, I'm sorry you walked in on that. That was never my intention, I swear. But mom, come on. I'm not your little man anymore. I'm seventeen, almost eighteen, and getting ready to figure out what I'm gonna do after high school. You had to know this day would come. I mean, even Des knew, and he gave me condoms so I would play it safe."

Not realizing how my words are affecting her, I keep going.

"I've been careful, and I've been safe, so there's nothing to worry about. Can I have this conversation with Des, please? He gets it, and this is so uncomfortable, not to mention embarrassing. "

"Jagger, you and I will be having a conversation after I speak to Des. For now, you're grounded from games, phone, and friends. You will go straight to school, then straight home. You're punishment isn't because you're having sex, even though I'm disappointed, but it's because you broke our rules. Son, look at me...I love you, and I know you're growing, and becoming your own man. As hard as that is, I get it, but—and this is huge—you have a younger sister, who for however long this has been going on, is in the same house. You are having sex with a girl *her* age in your bed. How can I tell her that when she decides to go there with a boyfriend, it has to mean something, when you're doing it with one of *her* friends?"

"Mom, Daisy and Sabrina aren't friends. I don't even think they like each other."

"Damn it, Jagger, I DON'T CARE! Something's been going on with your sister, and I don't think this is helping her at all.

44

We are done for now, but know that this isn't over. You get me, kid?"

"Yeah, mom. I get ya."

Dee Dee

I sit in the family room, waiting for Des to get home, and I am fuming. Where the hell does Des get off giving my son condoms? What the fuck was he thinking? He never even talked to me about it, or even mentioned it after the fact. I was blindsided by Jagger when he told me Des knew, and even provided the protection. I am so pissed; I feel like my head is going to explode. Des had no right, even if we are living together. These are my kids, and he shouldn't have gone behind my back to get in with my son. I know he thinks he is doing the right thing being the man. The last couple of months have been confusing for me because as much as I want Des to be a part of my kid's lives, I feel like I am losing some of them to him. And it has always been Jagger, Daisy and me.

The door opens and in walks Des. Seeing me, he starts to smile, then realizes something's up.

"Hey, baby. You okay?"

"No, *baby*, everything is not *okay*. When were you going to tell me that you gave Jagger condoms? My teenage son, who must have thought that meant it was okay for him to have sex. Well, guess what, Des, he's having sex in our home. When we're at work, while my fourteen-year-old daughter is in the room across the hall! Nice, real nice, Des."

By the look on his face, I can tell he didn't expect me to be so crazy about this, but he hasn't seen anything yet.

"I think we need to step back and take some time. Things are moving too fast. I have kids, Des, and I will say this once...these are *my* kids, not yours. So you don't get to tell them what to do, or give them things that could possibly hurt them. You run crap by me first because I am their mother. Are we clear?"

"Baby, calm the fuck down. I know you're upset, but come on! Jagger's almost eighteen. Did you think he wasn't gonna have sex until he got married? Really, Dee Dee? Did you wait until you got married? No, you didn't, so why would you expect your son, who's almost a man, to wait? I'm not trying to be a prick, but you're acting like a total bitch, and I don't deserve it. We're a family, and you're not gonna tie my hands behind my back when it comes to our kids. I didn't make them, but I love them, just as much as you do. Fuck, their own father doesn't care enough to be around, but I do. So let's sit down and talk about this like adults, okay? Come on baby."

Looking at the one and only man I have ever loved, I know he's right, but my brain doesn't agree. I am so mad that right now I want him gone.

"Get out. Please respect my wishes and go. Go back to your house, because right now, I don't want you here."

Taking a deep breath, I watch the struggle on his face.

"I love you, Dee Dee, and I'll respect your wishes, but know this, I won't wait forever. I also love those kids, and you know it." He turns and walks back out the door he just came in.

Feeling the tears start, I'm unaware of Jagger coming to sit by my side. Pulling me into his arms, he holds me tightly.

"Mom, don't be mad at Des. I went to him and we talked. Even though we had the 'sex talk' when I was younger, I needed a man's point of view. I don't want you to fight with Des over this sh...crap. It's my fault, so please call him and tell him to come home."

Watching my son break down, and knowing that Des didn't do anything wrong, I feel like such a bitch. But for some reason, at this moment, I can't call Des and tell him to come home.

I'm not sure why, I just know I can't.

Chapter 9

Wolf

Christmas Eve

The night everyone at Wheels & Hogs has been looking forward to has arrived. I look around my house, amazed at how fantastic it looks. The girls did a wonderful job of decorating by keeping it simple, yet masculine, if that's possible.

Going through the family room, I check out the dining area where the tables have been set up. Since the same folks that were at Thanksgiving will be coming here, we have multiple tables set up. Thank God my house has an open floor plan, and the rooms are huge. After checking on the tables, I go to the kitchen to see how the food's coming.

Fern's with Ann and Carol in the kitchen taking charge as usual, her maternal ways always shining brightly. The smells remind me of Christmas's past. As I enter, Fern's eyes catch mine, and she shoots me a smile with a twinkle in her eyes. Smiling back, I go to the center counter and grab a black olive from the lazy Susan. Ann goes to the fridge and pulls out a Rubbermaid, pushing it towards me.

"Eat these so we won't have to refill that tray. I love black olives too."

Taking the container with me, I look around, and man, these women have it all together. There are trays of Christmas cookies, fudge, breads, brownies, and other things I've never seen before, but I plan to try them all. The presentation is breathtaking. Yeah, I provided the house, but they did the rest. I start to feel bad because I didn't even ask if they needed anything.

"Fern, is there anything I can do to help? Guess it's kind of late to ask, but I have two willing hands here."

As I finish, Fern looks behind me with a smile on her face. Ann and Carol start to giggle, and I know I've put my foot in my mouth as I turn and see Willow in the doorway. She looks beautiful in a shiny red dress that fits her perfectly. Her long hair is in waves over her shoulder, and she's wearing a little bit of make-up, which only accents her beauty.

So absorbed in how amazing she looks, I don't realize that Fern is behind me, pushing me forward. She grins and says, "Mistletoe."

Shit. I look at Willow, and then glance up. Sure enough, hanging from the doorway is a bunch of mistletoe, directly above Willow's head. I now get why the women were grinning and acting silly. They all knew about Willow's crush, and thought they were helping. Can I do this? As much as I want to feel Willow under my hands and in my bed, I don't want to embarrass her either. Walking towards her, or rather being pushed towards her, Willow's eyes widen. She looks around, seeing the women's faces, then looks up and starts to giggle.

"Wolf, do you actually believe in mistletoe? Come on, everyone, jokes on me. I get it. You don't have to follow through, Wolf. So, what do you want me to do, Fern? I'm here early because I thought you could use a couple of extra hands."

Seeing her so nervous, I actually walk up to her and put my hands to her cheeks. She looks up at me, surprised, but also excited, which takes my breath away. It also affects other parts of my body. But Fern started it, so I need to see it through.

"*Hopa Cante Skuye*. Merry Christmas, Willow."

Lowering my head slowly, I watch the bluest eyes I've ever seen, stare back at me. I gently put my lips to hers, and kiss her slowly. I'm taken aback when I feel the tip of her tongue touch my lower lip. Something inside me feels the pull, and I take over the kiss. I open my lips, and to my surprise, Willow presses forward with her peppermint tasting tongue. As soon as hers touches mine, I pull her even closer to me as her arms wrap around my waist. This is my first taste of Willow, and I can't think of why I waited so fucking long. She feels like heaven in my arms. I move my hand to her hair, slanting my mouth over hers to get better access. I feel the moan from her mouth enter mine as our tongues tangle together, then I gently nibble her bottom lip. Her body trembles as I start to pull back, and she follows me, letting me know she doesn't want it to end. But, end it I do, as this is not the right time or place for this to continue. We have an audience. But damn, I'm all for getting to know my *Cante*. Holding her by the shoulders as I watch her struggle to find her balance, I hear the giggling behind us. Looking over my shoulder, all three of the ladies have huge smiles on their faces.

"Now that's what I call a mistletoe kiss. Can't wait for the bikers to get here. I'm gonna trap each and every one of them." Ann says before she begins to laugh hysterically.

I turn back to Willow. "Wow, woman. I'm still trying to catch my breath. That was some kiss, Willow."

She looks up at me and her cheeks are a pretty shade of pink. I release her just as the doorbell rings.

It's later in the evening, and I stand in the doorway off the kitchen, watching everything going on in my home. This is what the holidays are all about—family, friends, and children excited about Santa, who will bring them presents.

All the women are in the kitchen, getting everything ready. The phenomenal smells hit my senses, making my head swim. Between dinner, desserts, warm apple cider and eggnog with cinnamon, all those scents makes my stomach clench, letting me know how hungry I actually am.

"Uncle Woof, look at me! I'm under da mistletoe, but no one is kissing me. Why?" little Emma screeches. Moving quickly and quietly, I grab the little girl from behind, and give her a huge kiss on her pink little cheek. She starts to laugh, then wraps her hand around my neck to grab my braid, and holding onto it for dear life. She lifts up in my arms and gives me a kiss on my cheek.

"Uncle Woof! We are now married. We kissed each udder."

"Emma, Uncle Wolf kissed Auntie Willow first, so he would be married to her. He can't marry two girls at the same time, and he would fit better with her because they're both old," Charlie adds with a huge smile, making everyone laugh.

"I'll have you know, Charlie, that I'm not old, just older than you," Willow replies with a smile.

"Auntie Willow, you're the prettiest one here and I would marry you. Wanna kiss me?"

"Charlie, I would, but there's some lucky girl out there, who'll someday want to be your wife. So to keep you from breaking my heart in the future, let's stay friends, if that's okay with you?"

"Okay, Auntie Willow." Charlie heads towards the counter and grabs some snacks. No one's paying much attention until after he starts to cough, then he begins to choke.

"Oh my God, Charlie. Did you eat something with nuts in it? Crap. Honey, just breathe for me, nice and slow. Remember, in and out. Gramma's here." Ann looks up. "Gabriel, please grab my purse. I have an Epi pen in there. Charlie, relax. We'll get you all fixed up."

Everyone's looking for Ann's purse. Fern comes quickly from the back room, her purse in her hands, and pulls out the pen thingy, handing it over to Ann.

Fern's face shows the same worry as everyone else as Ann grabs her grandson and shoves his pants down before she pushes the small needle into his thigh. As she pushes down the top of the pen, it takes only a few seconds before Charlie starts to breathe easier, and the ruby red in his cheeks starts to lighten. Everyone takes a deep breath and moves away, except Carol, who's watching Ann, Fern, and Gabriel as they deal with the young child. Fern is crying softly when Charlie looks up, and begins wiping her tears away.

"Momma would cry too when I got sick. Fern, I'm okay. I'm sorry that I made you cry."

"Honey, there's nothing to be sorry about. We knew about your allergy to nuts, but not everyone here did. It's my fault for not letting them know how peanuts make you sick, lil man. It's nothing more than a bump in the road. How are you feeling now?"

"I'm hungry. When are we gonna eat? When Gramma gives me the shot, it works pretty fast, so I think I'm okay."

Carol walks over, truly upset, with her hands to her face as she tries to control herself.

"My God, Fern. I had no idea my dip had crushed nuts in it. I am so sorry."

Fern brings Charlie close to her with one hand on his head. "Carol, it's not your fault. Both Ann and I knew about his peanut allergy. We didn't even think to tell everyone. He's good, so let's just enjoy the evening. If you don't mind though, can we move your dish somewhere he can't reach it, just to be safe?"

As everyone continues with the final preparations, Fern and Ann grab each other, thankful that this didn't turn into something disastrous.

As we prepare to eat our Christmas Eve dinner, I watch my family—friends who have come to mean so much to me. My eyes drift to Willow, and I see her gazing back at me with a look in her eyes that makes my blood heat. As we continue to look at each other, everyone else slowly drifts away. Something's different about Willow since our kiss, and it's drawing me closer to her, even though I'm fighting it with every breath. As much as I want to move forward with her, my secrets hold me back. The biggest being the woman who held my heart for so long that even now the pain is fresh. My life is so complicated, and that's why I've never approached her. I don't want to hurt her, but at this moment, I want her with everything that makes me a man.

Chapter 10

Willow & Wolf

I'm stretching in a bed that isn't mine as the early morning light sneaks through the drapes. I pull my long hair up, clipping it in a messy bun. Knowing Archie's going to be pissed that even though she warned me, I stayed the night at Wolf's house. Hearing noise from the kitchen, I get up and go to the bathroom to wash my face and brush my teeth. I'm so grateful Wolf had an extra toothbrush. I head out of the guest bedroom to the kitchen in one of Wolf's T-shirts that fits me like a dress. It's way too large as it falls mid-thigh. Knowing that I'm acting like a schoolgirl with a crush makes me give myself a good shake.

Entering the kitchen, I see Wolf standing at the counter in a pair of low-cut jeans and a thermal that fits him like a glove. His waist long hair is loose, and seeing it for the first time like this, my fingers itch to run through the black shiny silk that brushes the top of his delectable ass. And to top it off, he's barefoot. For some reason, that moves him up a notch in my book to super sexy. Caught up in my ogling, I don't realize that he's turned, and sees me in the doorway.

"Willow. Good Morning, and Merry Christmas, *Hopa.* Would you like a cup of coffee, or maybe tea?"

Walking to him, I reach out and touch his cheek as he leans into my hand at the same time.

"Merry Christmas, Wolf. I would love some coffee if you have some made."

Shocking us both, I rise up on my toes and gently touch his cheek with my lips. I move slightly back and look around the room, seeing that the girls cleaned up pretty much everything last night. Since we're going to meet up at Des' house later for the visit from "Santa," we have time before we have to go. I should probably give Wolf some time, but I'm enjoying living out my fantasy.

"Take a seat, *Hopa*, and I'll get you some coffee. How do you take it, and can I fix you some breakfast? I was just getting started, so it will be easier to cook for two instead of one."

"Coffee with cream, and sure, I can eat. I eat just about anything, so whatever you're making is fine with me."

We talk as Wolf prepares our breakfast. I try to watch him from under my lashes so he doesn't catch me ogling him. God, he's beautiful. His long, silky black hair sways as he moves, and his lean torso is outlined by his thermal. His body is perfection, from head to toe. I can feel the saliva gathering at the sides of my lips. What the hell is the matter with me? Yes, I have always crushed on Wolf, but not to this extreme. In my own thoughts, I don't see Wolf as he approaches me, so I'm startled when his voice is so close to my ear. His breath brushes my cheek as he speaks.

"Try this, and let me know if you like it. It's something my mom used to make for Christmas, and it's always been one of my favorites this time of year."

Looking at the pastry he places in front of me, I carefully bite into the corner since it's still pretty warm. My mouth explodes with the flavors of vanilla and cinnamon on a flakey crust, with jam in the middle. This tastes like heaven.

"Wow. This is amazing. I can't believe how light it is, and with so many flavors."

I devour the pastry. When I finish, I realize something's changed. Licking my lips as I look up, I find Wolf focusing on me, a serious expression on his face. Suddenly, it seems as if the air is being sucked out of the room. I feel heat in my chest, moving up my neck and to my cheeks. What's happening? I watch as he straightens, making me feel so small in front of him. Time passes as we continue to stare at each other. My breath comes in short gasps. An unknown energy is pulling me to him, and he hasn't uttered a word. As I slowly move towards him, he stays in place, making no attempt to meet me halfway. It feels like he's speaking to me with no words, and my body understands the conversation. Once I'm standing right in front of him, I shiver at the intensity of his gaze.

"*Cante Skvye*, be very sure of your next actions. I am not like the boys you tend to attract, and that is why I have stayed away. I am a man, Willow, a very demanding one. Once I see something I want, I will not give up. This will be the only warning I give to you. No games, *Hopa*."

My body is on fire, and the wetness between my legs is going down my inner thighs. My panties are soaked, and he hasn't even touched me. His voice holds so much authority. Wolf takes one finger, and runs it up and down my arm. Goosebumps immediately cover my body as I gasp. He appears to smirk at my reaction as he moves his other arm up to caress my face. I tilt into his hand and feel a calm that I have never felt before. Serenity is the feeling that comes to mind.

"Willow, look at me. Tell me you want this. I've been fighting it for years, but now that you're within my reach, I no longer have the will to fight it, but I need to hear you say it, *Hopa*. Tell me this is what you want, because once I start, I won't be able to stop."

His eyes that are looking at me like he can see into my soul mesmerize me. I don't have strength to utter a word. I feel a need that I have never felt before. So, doing the only thing I can, I move closer and lift up on my toes, and press my lips to his.

The firmness of his lips is in contrast to the intensely soft feel of them. It only lasts for a few seconds, but as I start to pull away, I can feel his energy surround me. He pulls me to him, roughly, and slams his lips down on mine. A sudden tingling takes over my entire body. At the touch of his tongue on my lips, I let him in. His hands are running up and down the sides of my body, then one hand grabs my hair, moving my head this way and that way, as he continues to devour my mouth. His kiss is hard, wet, and so sexual, I never want it to end. When I go to touch him, he stops me, holding both arms at my sides. I feel powerless, but safe. It's confusing, but wonderful at the same time. I let Wolf have his way, and never before have I felt so wanted, needed and at the same time taken care of. His mouth moves to my neck, where he bites down on the skin between my neck and collarbone. I gasp as I feel it right down to my core. I try to move in closer, just as someone knocks on the door. We both turn, still wrapped around one another, when the door opens, and Prudence walks in with a huge smile on her face. That is until she sees us together. The smile becomes shaky as she puts the gifts in her hands on Wolf's counter.

"Oh shit! I am so sorry. I didn't mean to interrupt. I wanted to drop these off before the day got away. Merry Christmas, Wolf."

As she turns to leave, Wolf unexpectedly lets me go, but not before he makes sure I'm stable on my feet.

"Prudence, stop. Give me a minute to explain."

She turns with tears in her eyes, giving me a strange look before turning her attention to Wolf.

"Nothing to explain. I get it, Wolf. Always have, and it's nice to see you finally get what you want."

Wolf drops his head, and without another word, she turns and leaves, closing the door behind her.

I'm in shock, not sure what just happened. What has he not told me? It's obviously something big, and all I can do is stand here, feeling lost, out of sorts and in the dark.

Chapter 11

Dee Dee

Christmas Morning with Des & Dee Dee

Smelling coffee, I try to pry my eyes open, but fail...not once, but twice. Finally, when I'm able to peek through my lashes, I see Des standing at the side of the bed with a steaming cup of coffee and a sexy smile. As I stretch, my body feels the wonderful effects from our tryst last night, after we left Wolf's house. Des' mouth, hands, and body know how to make mine sing.

"Morning, babe. Sleep good?"

With the sexy grin lighting up his face, he already knows the answer to that. I'm so relaxed I don't want anything to ruin this feeling.

"Merry Christmas, Des. I feel great. Are the kids up yet?"

Shaking his head, he places the mug on the nightstand before he lies down on top of me, giving me his weight.

"Not really. Jagger's up, but still in his room with the door closed. Daisy, well, I have no idea, Dee Dee. She's not even excited about Christmas this year, and I'm still not sure what the fuck's going on with her. We need to figure it out, 'cause that's not our kid in there."

I feel my body tighten at his words. My kids are mine, but whenever he refers to them as ours, I feel a wonderful emotion that I can't describe, which is more than their biological father has ever given me.

"Let's not start this today, Des. She's a teenage girl, going through the normal growing pains of being a teenager. I've been keeping an eye on her, but today we celebrate Christmas with our family and friends. I don't want anything to knock over the apple cart, if you know what I mean. With this being Charlie and Emma's first Christmas without their mom, I want it to be perfect for them. Okay?"

"I know that, babe. Fuck, you've been baking and cooking for what seems like weeks. I think I've gained ten to fifteen pounds with all those damn cookies you made. As good as they are, I can't wait until they're gone. But right now, we need to get down to business. I want to fuck you before we start the day, so are you gonna give me some Christmas lovin'?"

Reaching up, I grab him by the hair and pull him down. Our lips touch, and instantly, the hunger is there. As Des' tongue tangles with mine, his hands start to caress my breasts, then he rolls my nipples between his fingers. Every time he does this, I feel a rush of wetness between my legs. His mouth leaves mine to trail to my neck, where he rubs his stubble up and down to my pleasure. I moan as his mouth trails down to my nipples, blowing gently on them as I gasp at the sensation. I lift my hips, wanting to feel his hardness. Between his fingers and mouth, he's driving me crazy. His hands move down, and before I can take a breath, his fingers find my sweet spot. He begins rubbing circles around my clit, and before I know it, my body tightens as my orgasm takes hold of me. My need and desire for him is unraveling me. I start to push my hips up and down as he lays on top of me, trying to get his cock right where I need it. As I reach for him, I lose my hold when he moves from me and gets off the bed. I watch as he reaches behind his neck, grabs his shirt, and impatiently pulls it over his head. My eyes take in his torso, covered in muscle and tattoos, and my mouth waters as he reaches down to unbutton his jeans. As they fall from his narrow hips, I see he's commando. His hard, long cock is pointing up at his stomach, pre-cum leaking from the tip.

"Baby, you want a taste? Come on, open wide and let me in. I wanna feel that soft, warm mouth on my cock as I fuck your face. We don't have a lot of time, so take it now."

I oblige, opening my mouth at his request. As soon as his taste hits my tongue, I close my lips around the head and suck gently. Once I take him in slowly, I run my tongue around the ridge, along the vein, and pull him all the way in. I feel his body tense as I move up and down, loving the feel of his cock in my mouth. I cup his balls and squeeze gently. I feel his hands in my hair, holding me back so he can watch. I want to give him a good show. I bring him all the way in, to the back of my throat. I swallow and moan, letting the sensation take him over. His hands tighten as his body starts to shake. Knowing this is getting to him, I bring his cock almost all the way out, but leave the tip still inside. My tongue goes around the head, and I look up, seeing the lust in his eyes as he stops me and pulls me up his body. As soon as he has me on top of him, he rolls us and begins removing my clothes. Once they're gone, he gently cups my face as he thrusts into me, hard and fast. My legs wrap around his waist as my hands run up and down his back with my nails leaving marks everywhere. My hands land on his tight ass as I grab his cheeks pulling him even closer to me. Trying to keep the noise down, Des plants his mouth on mine, just as I feel the familiar tightness in my entire body coming way too quickly. He knows, so he grinds down, and then rounds his hips making contact with my clit. Shit. That's all it takes to for me to moan out my release. As I tighten around him, he loses his rhythm but continues to thrust fast and deep a couple of times, then he cums inside of me.

This was the perfect way to start our Christmas celebration.

As I watch my family opening their gifts on this snowy Christmas morning, I realize how far we have come. Des has taken to my children, as they have to him. I finally have what I've always wanted—a real family. I have a man who has my back, and loves not only me, but also my kids.

Jagger's enjoying opening each gift, even if some things are things that he needed, and not what he wanted. Daisy opens her gifts with no excitement or joy. I notice that this is the first year all the gifts from her are store bought. Usually my girl makes unique homemade gifts for all of us.

Des takes my attention away from the kids as he comes towards me with my gifts. He places them by my feet and sits next to me. I decide to open the big box first, but when I reach for it, Des has to give me a hand because it's heavier than I'd thought. Ripping off the wrapping paper, I'm shocked to see a box that says Mac Pro. It's a new laptop! I look to Des, who's smiling, then to the kids, who to my utter shock, have huge grins on their faces.

"Des, we did it. She looks surprised."

Jagger laughingly states. Then I hear Daisy.

"Jagger's right, Des. She's speechless, and that's a first. We got you, Mom."

Des looks to the kids and nods his head, and then back to me, with so much emotion in his eyes, I'm taken aback.

"Merry Christmas, baby. That's from all of us. We know yours is a piece of shit, so Jagger did the research, then Daisy and I went to get it. It's supposed to have all the good stuff you need, and we got you the training to go with it 'cause it's a Mac, and your last one was a Windows type. Hope you like it."

I put the box down next to me and grab Des, giving him a hard kiss right on the lips that leads to our tongues touching. I can hear the kids in the background with 'gross,' and 'come on,' but I give it to him good, then I rush my kids, giving each a kiss on their cheeks.

I'm in total shock. This truly is the best Christmas ever. Not because of the laptop, even though it's an awesome gift, but because of the relationship I have with Des and my kids. These relationships mean the most to me. I finally feel like life is going the way I have always wanted it to. I'm humbled, and so very happy.

Chapter 12

Des

Christmas Dinner

Soon, everyone will be arriving, but I need to do this before they get here. I knock on Daisy's door, waiting for her to tell me to come in. I get nothing, so I assume she's listening to her new iPod with her ear buds in. Opening the door slowly, I see her laying on the bed, head bobbing to the music. There's no doubt this girl loves her music. Walking to the bed, I put my hand on her shoulder. She jumps from the bed like a scared cat. What the fuck is this?

"Daisy, got a minute? I need to talk to you."

She takes a few deep breaths before putting the iPod down, sitting up on the edge of her bed.

"Yeah, Des. What's up?"

"Baby girl, come on. You know what's up. We've been having this dance for a while now, and you know your mom is worried sick. I just want to check in and see how you're doin'. Also, I want to make sure you know you can come to me anytime, and we can talk about anything—always. No judgment from me."

Her face shows so much sorrow as her shoulders start to shake, then tears start to run down her cheeks. This is not my territory. What made me think today was the day to try and get whatever is bothering her out?

"Come here, baby girl. It's gonna be okay. There's nothin' that should cause you to be this sad. You have all of us behind you, so let it out. Give it to Des."

I hold her tight as she lets all of her pent up frustrations out, crying quietly in my arms. She may not be ready to talk, but I hope it will help her get through today. She needs to know that she can tell us anything, and whatever it is she's going through, she doesn't have to take it out on the people who love her. I pat her on the back of her head as she slowly starts to calm down.

"Sorry, Des. I don't know what came over me. Please don't tell Mom. She'll freak out, and I don't want to ruin her Christmas."

I look down into her amber eyes that are so like her mother's, and understand that she trusts me, so I give it to her straight.

"Daisy, I'll not speak about this to your mom, for now, but I want you to promise me that you'll come to me and tell me what the hell is going on with you. It doesn't have to be today, or tomorrow, but when you feel you're ready to talk to us about it. Is that a deal?"

She looks up at me with tears on her beautiful face and smiles.

"Deal. Merry Christmas Des, love you. Thanks for caring."

"Awe, honey. You don't have to thank me for lovin' you. You're just so lovable."

She looks at me for a moment, then a small giggle bursts from her lips, and I swear, it's the best Christmas gift I could ever receive from her, and that's her trust.

The entire Christmas table is crowded with family, friends, and the Horde. I raise my glass after getting the cue from Dee Dee. I clink my fork against my glass to get everyone's attention.

"Hey, settle down. Before I give the Christmas toast, I'm gonna ask Charlie to say Grace."

Watching the little boy get red in the face as he crosses himself with a huge smile on his face, I look to Gabriel, who's watching him, but gives me a quick glance and smiles, which lets me know that he's glad I remembered. The kid's mom always said Grace before meals, and we all want to keep her memory with her children alive, especially around the holidays.

After Charlie finishes, I raise my glass high in the air. "First and foremost, a thank you to our Lord for getting us all here in one piece. I'm so grateful this year for each and every one of you, as this year has been a rough one. Merry Christmas to everyone here, and I hope we're all around next year to celebrate the holidays again, together. May we always remember that Christmas is about family and friends, and not gifts, trees, and decorations? Merry Christmas."

People begin clinking their glasses together, wishing each other a Merry Christmas. The atmosphere is lively and joyous as we start our holiday dinner. We have four tables packed with our family. Even Axe, Bear, Ugly, Stash, and Enforcer showed up.

As I sit back, my plate full of all the fixings, the love around the table overwhelms me. I look up and see Dee Dee looking around the table, with a beaming smile on her beautiful face. Candles light the table and reflect off her amber eyes as they look over to me. She mouths, "I love you," and I repeat the same to her. Finally, I feel like I have everything I've ever wanted. Daisy, who's watching her mom and I, blinds me with one of her gorgeous smiles. It truly lights up the whole damn room.

Life is good in the Connelly home today.

As dinner starts to come to an end, Fern gets up and grabs an envelope of some sorts off the counter. She looks to Gabriel, who puts his fingers to his lips and whistles. Everyone immediately quiets down.

"Fern wants to start a new tradition for Christmas, and no complaining, or you answer to me. Go ahead, Sugar."

Fern clears her throat.

"When I was a little girl, my grandparents always passed the Oplatek at Christmas. It's a Polish tradition where we'd share the wafer while telling each other what we're grateful for in our lives. If everyone is open to it, I would love to start this tradition today, as I think we all have a lot to be thankful for."

She looks around the table with such hopefulness in her eyes, that no one in their right mind would even consider telling her no. When everyone agrees, her face beams with so much joy.

"Great! I'll start. All you do is break a piece off and say what you're thankful for, then you eat it." She glances at Wolf and Axe. "I don't think it's against anything you guys believe in, but if you aren't comfortable with the wafer, you can just tell us what you're grateful for."

They both nod with small smiles on their faces. Fern is always considerate of everyone's ways.

"Well, I'm thankful for my life. This year, going through cancer, I wasn't sure I would make it. Dying didn't scare me, but leaving all of you did, especially my Gabriel. That is what I'm grateful for."

As Fern takes a small piece and puts it in her mouth, she passes the envelope to Ann, who has tears in her eyes.

"For me, I am thankful for each and every one of you. Losing Lydia was the hardest thing I've ever been through, but the Horde made it bearable. And for the way you love my grandchildren and me, I thank you all. No words can express how much it means."

Sniffles can be heard across the tables as Ann takes a piece and passes it to Charlie.

"I am thankful for Gramma, Fern, and Gabriel for loving me. Also for my sissy and all of you. And for all the presents under the tree."

He takes a huge piece and shoves it in his mouth, handing the envelope to Emma.

"I'm tankful dat God made room in 'is ouse for Mommy, and dat we ave a mommy, Daddy, and Gramma who takes care of Tarlie and me." Ann and Fern are crying, and Gabriel's struggling to keep it together.

Eating a piece, she gives it to Wolf who looks at it for a bit. "I am thankful to the Great Spirit for bringing all of you into my life. It has never been fuller, or had more meaning." Taking just a sliver, he puts it on his tongue and passes the rest to Cadence.

"For Trinity giving me a second chance, and for the birth of our daughter Hope. For all of you, sticking by me, when I was at my worst."

As the envelope is passed around, we all listen to what everyone has to be thankful for. It's humbling to know how much we care for each other. Finally, it makes its way to the table where the bikers sit. Never knowing what to expect, Ugly takes a corner of the wafer and smells it, and the kids giggle. He seems to be thinking, then looks up.

"I'm thankful to be alive and sitting at this table with the finest group of people I have had the pleasure of knowing. My life hasn't always had purpose, but getting to know all of you gives me something to reach for. Thanks."

He bends his head as Archie reaches over and gives him a pat on the shoulder, then gets up and puts an innocent kiss on his cheek. His face turns red as everyone gives him shit, but if they were looking close enough, they would see how intently he's looking at Archie.

Finally, the last person grabs the envelope, and it's Enforcer. His looks are scary enough, but his voice sounds like he smokes a pack of cigarettes a day. His size is so intimidating that people always give him a wide berth. He looks around the tables with an unreadable look, until he settles it on Fern. He gets up and walks over to her, giving her a kiss on the cheek. Breaking off some of the wafer, he holds it up.

"I'm thankful for this beautiful woman who brought back a childhood memory I had all but forgotten. This is a tradition my mom did every Christmas. We were poor, but she wanted to bring us up right, realizing that we might not have everything, but we had what was important. Thanks, Fern, for bringing that back for me. Merry Christmas to each of you. You're my family now, and I'm proud to call ya that."

Fern is looking around the room with tears running down her face. Gabriel gets up and pulls her to him and begins whispering in her ear.

"Thanks, everyone, for giving a woman the dream of a lifetime—her family together at Christmas. This means the world to me." Fern curls closer into Gabriel.

Everyone stands and starts to clean the kitchen up as Gabriel and Fern share a quiet moment together until Charlie and Emma run over and get in on the hug

Chapter 13

Des

Christmas Visit from Santa

As everyone sits in our great room, looking at the massive tree and all the gifts underneath, I'm giving the stink eye to Wolf and Cadence to follow me into the den.

"Where in the fuck is Santa? Dee Dee's gonna lose her shit if he doesn't show up at the right time."

Both Wolf and Cadence smile, but I don't see anything funny.

"Des, calm down. They're trying to get Bear in the red suit. He's a bit on the larger side, and it's gonna be a tight fit. Not that he's a fat dude, but those muscles might be a bit too big for the costume." Cadence finishes on a laugh.

"This year has been especially hard on Emma and Charlie, so Dee Dee wants to give them something positive for the holidays and good memories, as they're both young enough and still believe. And you know that whatever Dee Dee wants, I give to her."

Cadence snorts under his breath. "Pussy whipped." I crack him in the side of his head.

"Like you're not. The only one here that isn't is Wolf, and that's because he doesn't have a woman. Cadence, go see how much longer before the dude in the red suit shows up."

I watch as the kid drags his feet to the front door, and hear a chuckle coming from Wolf, who's trying to hold in his laughter.

I can't believe it's been more than thirteen years since I first saw him in that bar. Time truly flies by.

"So, when are you going to join the club and be whipped, Wolf? 'Cause I'm not likin' standing here while you grin like the cat that ate the canary. What, no woman good enough for ya? I can name a few who'd do just about anything to be in that line, and some of them you know quite well. So what's the hold up?"

He whispers words I never thought would come from his mouth. "Des, I can't start a relationship with anyone. I'm still married."

The shock of his words almost knock me on my ass, and his face looks like he can't believe he even said it out loud. Before I can question him, I hear Cadence bellowing loudly from the front door.

"Kids, you will never believe who's outside on his sled. That's right, Santa's here with his reindeer."

"Damn it already. Where is everyone? Umph. What the fuck, Ugly. Why did you…Oh shit…I mean, Ho Ho Ho. Merry Christmas, kids. Come on over and meet my reindeer.

With my arms wrapped around Dee Dee, she gabs with Fern, who is wrapped in Gabriel's arms. I turn my attention to all the women of the Horde. The kids are having a blast, even the older ones, as the bikers, along with Santa, empty out a bag full of presents. Charlie's looking at Santa in awe as he tentatively touches his red suit. Emma's sitting next to Santa in the sled, blown away just as much as her brother. She keeps looking to Ann, and then back to Santa, not believing her own eyes. Jagger and Daisy are playing along so the kids can have their best Christmas.

Pulling Dee Dee in closer, I lean close and whisper, "You happy, Baby?"

She nods her head and I smile. Mission accomplished. All I want to do now is kick back and enjoy the rest of the day with my friends and family. We were all due this time, so I plan to make the most of it.

This is what the season is truly about, the little things that mean the world to everyone, and for me, everyone I care about is right here, enjoying their time with Santa.

As I look around, I start to laugh hysterically, as both Cadence and Wolf approach Bear, or Santa as he's still in his costume, to sit on his lap and tell him what they wanted and didn't get. He looks like he's ready to run.

And that's how the Horde enjoys their time together, keeping it real, even with Santa Claus.

Chapter 14

Cadence

Planning a Surprise Wedding

With Trinity assuming I'm at work, I head over to Wolf's to meet everyone. We have under a week to pull this off now that Christmas is over. I'm a nervous wreck, and trying to keep my mouth shut is really hard.

Secrets usually don't last long with me, my mouth always giving them away, so at the moment, Trinity thinks I'm mad at her 'cause I'm barely speaking to her. Even Hope thinks something's wrong. The girls took Hope dress shopping without Trinity, but didn't buy the dress until Hope was back at home. Hope tells her momma everything, including every one of my curse words for the swear jar.

Pulling into Wolf's long drive, I can't believe that I'm getting married this Friday. I never thought I would get married, or have a child, in less than a couple of years, but look at me now; all grown up and being responsible. How the hell did all this happen?

Getting out of the truck, I head to the door, which opens immediately, and Charlie runs out.

"Cadence! I'm still the ring bearer, right?"

"Yeah, 'lil dude, you are. How's it going in there? They crazy yet?" He nods and giggles with me as we walk through the door.

"Holy shit," I get out before Emma screams.

"Momma Furn! C said a bad word." She looks at me and smiles her cute smile.

I smile back. She can't pronounce my name, so everyone told her to call me C.

"Sorry, baby girl. Just shocked at the house. It looks awesome."

And it does. Besides the Christmas tree, all other holiday decorations have been replaced with wedding decorations. Twinkling white lights are everywhere, along with white bows, mixed with the emerald green and light purple, the color the girls picked for the wedding, since they're Trinity's favorite. Throughout the house are wedding bells, white puffy doves, and vases with glittery crystals and shit. I have no idea where the furniture is, as they're in the process of putting some kind of runner down with our initials on it. Folded tables and chairs are against the walls.

I walk towards the kitchen, looking through the huge patio doors, and holy shit! It looks like a dream come true. Around the gazebo is a shimmery fabric, covering top to bottom with one side pulled back. Twinkling lights and vines are wrapped around it, and another runner, still rolled up, is waiting to be placed, I assume the day of the wedding. There are more chairs outside, waiting to be set up too.

According to the weather, Friday's supposed to be around forty-five to fifty during the day. Since we're doing this after sunset, the stars will be shining down on us. I'm sure it'll be a bit brisk, but that's okay.

"Got an idea, so let me know your thoughts. I have four outside heaters that I was thinking of putting out that night—two by the gazebo, and two on either side of the chairs. Should help keep everyone warm. What d'ya think?" Wolf asks.

I feel overwhelmed, and Wolf can see it. He reaches around me, pulling open the patio door, and turns to tell the women we'll be outside for a bit.

As we walk towards the gazebo, I'm suddenly scared to death. What in the fuck was I thinking? All this work, and what if Trinity doesn't want to get married? I'll look like an asshole, and all that money spent would be for nothing. Feeling nauseous, I lean over and grab my legs, trying to breathe deeply.

"Brother, it's okay to feel nervous. If you didn't, I would think something was wrong with ya. Just remember that Trinity loves being with you, and this will be the best surprise you have ever given her. It shows that you are totally committed to her and Hope. Follow your heart, Cadence, and it will be fine. I got your back…you know that, right?"

Nodding, I slowly stand straight, and once I'm up, Wolf grabs me and gives me a man hug. As crazy at it sounds, this is exactly what I need—my family and their support.

"Wolf, thanks for being here. Don't know what I'd do without you, brother. I feel calmer now. I'm just nervous that Trinity might not like what we've done, or even want to get married to me on Friday. My insecurities are playing with my head, but I'm sure it's all good."

We stay outside for a little longer so I can check out the pole barn, which is simply breathtaking. We then head back inside to make sure everything's set. The work they have all put into our special night is something I will never forget. Even my family is here, my mom and two brothers. Nothing has ever felt so right. Nothing.

Chapter 15

Trinity & Cadence

Thursday Arrives

Trinity

I wake to the feeling of someone watching me. Peeling my eyelids apart, I immediately see Cadence staring at me with a look I've never seen on his face before. Rubbing my eyes to clear the sleep, I lean into his chest, looking into those dark eyes that I love so much.

"Morning, honey. What's up? Something on your mind?"

He reaches out and cups my cheek with his hand, gently bringing his other hand to my ass and giving it a squeeze.

"All is good, Trin. just lots going on at work. We're so fuckin' busy, and I feel like I have no energy or time to spend with you and Hope. Not to mention, we need to find a house before the baby's born."

His hand moves from my ass to touch my tummy. We didn't plan to get pregnant so soon after Hope, but it's a miracle, no matter what. We're happy for our family to grow, and Hope is super excited for a little brother or sister. This pregnancy will be so different than the first, as Cadence has been a part of it since the very beginning. He's so looking forward to the baby's first kicks, and watching my belly grow. At least this time, the morning sickness and hormones aren't as bad.

"Can you talk to Des? Maybe get someone to help you with your workload? I hate to see you so strung out, being pulled in so many different directions. Is there anything I can do for you?"

"No, babe. It should calm down by this weekend. It's New Year's Eve tomorrow, and I know the Horde are going to Wolf's. You up to it?"

I hear what he's saying, but he seems nervous, like my answer will make or break him. Something's definitely up, and I'm going to get to the bottom of it. We swore no more secrets, since they can do so much damage.

"Cadence, you can tell me anything. What's going on? I can take it, I swear. I'm not the scared and weak little girl you met in the bar a couple years ago. I've grown up, a lot, and I can handle anything except a lie, so just tell me."

Instead of fessing up, he gives me one of his sexy smiles I usually get before he starts loving on me. I feel the familiar tingles, and when he pulls me on top of him, I feel my breasts swell, as my nipples get hard. His hand is on my ass, pulling me into his embrace as he pushes up with his hips, letting me feel how affected he is by my closeness. He's so hard, I can feel the piercings lining his cock, and I can't keep from biting my lip. Damn, can he turn me on with a look. It doesn't help that I'm far enough into my pregnancy that my hormones have me in a constant state of arousal. What's worse is that Cadence knows this.

"Come on, babe. You know I can't be this close to you and not have ya. Before we start, is Hope still sleeping? I won't be able to stop like the other day. That almost killed me."

I giggle because what he's talking about was really funny. Well, at least to me. We were going at it, hot and heavy, and I was enjoying the taste and feel of his cock with all his piercings, when Hope decided she was done napping. She started crying and screaming for both of us, and we could hear her clearly through the baby monitor. Looking up from between Cadence's

84

legs, I could see he was actually thinking of ignoring her. It had pissed me off, and I jumped off the bed and grabbed his flannel. I went to get my princess while listening to him whining in the background about blue balls and such. By the time I reached Hope's room, I was laughing at what a goof he could be.

"Yeah, she's still down. Its way too early for her to get up so…what do you have in mind?"

Without a word, his hands start to roam as he begins licking my lips until I open them for him. He makes quick work of removing my pants and shirt, all the while touching and caressing my body. Feeling warmth between my legs and the short breaths escaping my lips, he moves to my neck to the erogenous spot behind my ear, proving how well he knows my body. My hands reach between us and I shove my hand into his briefs, grasping onto his cock. Moving my hand around, I put pressure on his piercings. He moans loudly in my ear and thrusts his hips so I can get a better grip.

Our hands, lips, and tongues are everywhere, feeding the fire that's consuming us. As I start to move down to take him into my mouth, he surprises me by flipping us over, giving him the top position.

"Relax, Trinity. I want to make love to you, slowly."

He moves down my body and begins stroking his fingers up and down, right to my center. He uses his thumb to rub my swollen bud, and inserts two fingers inside of me, making me gasp. God, he makes me crazy. I move my hips, trying to match his rhythm, but he stops me.

"Don't move, not yet. Just enjoy it."

Feeling the need to move overwhelms me, but what he starts to do with his hands and his mouth feels so incredibly good, I fight to stay still. He moves up and takes my nipple into his mouth, licking and nipping, before moving to the other. His hands stay between my legs, hitting all the right spots, while his thumb continues to tease me until all I can do is gasp.

"Oh God, Cadence. Please don't stop. I need—ohhh I need...please don't stop."

I feel his hand move away, and as I open my mouth to protest, I feel his breath first, then his tongue, sucking and licking my swollen clit. My legs open wider and I press my hands to my mouth. As he continues to lick me, the pressure builds, and I can't hold back.

"Yes! That's it, right there. Ohhh fuck, oh God, I'm ahhhhhhhh."

He moves his tongue to my entrance, pushing it in and swirling it around, just as my orgasm starts. The feeling is too much, but not enough. As my orgasm goes on, he slides up my body and I open my eyes to see him gazing at me, his expression so full of love. We stare at each other and without breaking eye contact he enters me, taking my breath away. He's so hard, and his piercings are hitting all the right spots. I wrap my arms and legs around him and kiss him, tasting myself on his tongue. I love that we have no limits in our lovemaking.

"Touch yourself, Trin. I don't know how long I can last, but I need to feel you come, baby."

I move my hand between us as Cadence grabs the headboard. As soon as my fingers hit my clit, he starts to pound into me, hard and fast, with short strokes, then longer, harder strokes. I feel it as I tip over the edge again, screaming his name.

"Fuck! I'm gonna cum, Trin—oh shit!"

Thrust after thrust, he doesn't slow down until he's completely spent. We're both breathing heavy, and he keeps pushing inside of me, making our orgasms seem to go on forever. When he finally stops and pulls out, he lies on his side and pulls me close.

"Whatever happens, know this, Trinity Vinkers. I love you with my entire heart and soul. Always will, babe."

Feeling like he's trying to tell me something that I'm just not getting, and not wanting to ruin the moment, I let it go with no questions.

"I love you too, Cadence. I will for the rest of my life."

Chapter 16

Wolf

Wedding Day has Arrived - Wolf's House

Never have I been so happy for two people as I am for Cadence and Trinity. Today is the day of their wedding, and they deserve all the wonderful things that life has to offer, and I will do everything I can to make sure that happens.

The doorbell rings. As I go to answer it, I wonder who would be here this early. I haven't even started the coffee yet. Opening the door I see Prudence, appearing nervous as she looks around behind me. Seeing it's clear, I guess, she forces her way in, telling me to close the door.

"Pru, what's the matter? You seem shaken?"

"Wolf, I don't even know how to tell you this, but…oh crap! Of all days, it would have to be the day of the wedding."

Lightly touching her shoulder, as not to freak her out, I slowly pull her to me. With her past, being kept as a slave, I have to be very careful on any contact I have with her.

"Prudence, take a breath and try to relax. What has you so worried? You know you can trust me."

"Wolf, he found me…master found me, and that means we can finally find out what happened to Star! Wolf, we might find your Star."

Feeling the sweat start to run down my back, I push away from Prudence, needing some air. I open the door to go out onto my deck, and run right into Cadence, who was just about to knock. Fuck, not today!

"Wolf, dude, what the fuck's the matter? Is something wrong with the wedding plans? You have to tell me 'cause it has to be perfect."

Watching him, I flashback to another time and place, when I was the nervous groom wanting everything just so for my bride to be. Shaking the memory off, I turn and walk back into the house with Cadence following behind me. Prudence is wringing her hands together, tears running down her face. Seeing her, Cadence turns to me and bellows, "What the fuck is going on?"

"Cadence, calm down. We just got some bad news, personal news that has upset Pru. Give us a moment and we'll be fine. Can you do that, brother?"

"Got coffee made?" At my nod, he looks at me intently, then to Prudence before shrugging his shoulders and going into the kitchen. I can hear cabinets shutting, so I can only assume he's looking for the coffee. Looking directly at Prudence, I say my piece.

"Pru, honey, let's not go down that road today. He can't get to you or hurt you any longer. I swear it on my life, okay?" I wait for her response, then continue on. "As far as Star, that has been over for a very long time. She made a choice, and even though I have tried to find her to bring her back to her family, the relationship we had is dead. I want nothing to do with that woman ever again. So please, try to accept that so we can all move on."

For the first time ever, Prudence walks up to me and gives me a light hug. Shocked beyond belief, I freeze. With what she's gone through, this type of affection is beyond anyone's wildest dream and I know every detail.

"I wasn't thinking, Wolf. I'm so sorry to have brought her up to you, especially today, as I am sure a part of you hurts with the occasion we will be celebrating today. Know I am here for you, and will do whatever I can to help you. I can never repay you or Axe for all you have both done for me."

At the mention of my brother's name, her cheeks turn a pretty pink, and her eyes look everywhere but at me. *Interesting.* I smile down at her and hug her back. Damn, I'm glad that drama is over, for now.

We finally get back on track. With coffee in hand, Cadence and I go out to the backyard to check out the process of setting up for the nuptials. There are men and women, all doing different jobs, from rolling out the runner, and setting up chairs. We decided on the outside heaters, so I went and bought two more so we had a total of six. They should keep the chill off of everyone. The flower lady is starting to arrange the flowers around the gazebo. Everything is starting to come together.

Cadence walks around like he's in a daze. It's funny to watch, so I lean against the house and watch him trip over his own feet while checking everything out. Hearing the screen door open, I look to see both Dee Dee and Willow coming towards me. Damn, ever since that kiss, I see Willow so differently, and that in itself could be dangerous. Both women give me a kiss on the cheek, but Willow seems to linger a bit, and I think she actually sniffed me. Really? I chuckle to myself and wait to hear what they have to say.

"Oh Wolf it's so beautiful, don't you think? I tried to explain it to Des, but he's such a guy, never looking outside of the box. He isn't anything like you, Wolf. You see everything."

Looking at Dee Dee, I figure I snoozed too long. We're great friends, but it could have been more if I had just made a move. But then again, with Dee Dee comes the entire package including her kids. Now I love children, just as long as they aren't mine. With my past, it scares the shit out of me to even think of fathering a child. It's nice to play and spoil them, but I get to send them home. Although if I was with Dee Dee, that might not have been such a big chore. I watched both Daisy and Jagger grow up, and they are great kids. When it came down to it though, I didn't want to take the chance of it not working out, and losing her friendship, which means more to me than anything. We both like to tease and goad Des, but that's all it is.

"Dee Dee, why are you so surprised? You're the one who pulled this all together. I swear, sometimes you confuse the hell out of me."

I hear Willow giggle as Dee Dee turns her attention to me with a huge smile on her face.

"You're right, Wolf, but we all pulled it together. And the offer is out there. When you decide to plan your nuptials someday, my services will be offered to you and the lucky lady."

"Thanks for the offer, but that's never gonna happen. I don't need a piece of paper or a big party to show someone I care."

I glance at Willow to see the disappointment on her face as she lowers her head, but not before I see the tears in her eyes. Great, another woman I've managed to disappoint.

Chapter 17

Cadence and Trinity

Trinity's Surprise Spa Day

Cadence

Walking into the house, I see that Trinity is not having a good day. One of the cats must've had a bellyache 'cause there's puke all over the throw blanket on our leather couch. Hope's on the floor, chasing the cats, trying to catch them by their tails as Trinity tells her to stop. Knowing that it's time to let her in on my surprise, I feel nervous as hell. I can't tell her everything, obviously. I just need to tell her what she needs to know at the moment.

"Hey, babe. Cats sick again? You shouldn't be cleaning that up while you're pregnant. Let me get it."

She turns to me with a nasty look on her face. "I'm pregnant, not dying. I can do it. Grab your daughter and put her in her highchair. I need to get her fed."

I grab Hope, who seems to have lots of energy today. I put her in the highchair and place the plate in front of her with some baby food, mixed with some fruit.

"Babe, got a surprise for you. Come here."

"What did you do now?"

"Hey now, I was thinking about you and got you this. The girls will meet you there."

She looks at the gift card from the spa that they go to for their nail shit. It's a full spa from what Archie told me, so I

booked Trinity for a Mani/Pedi and a style, or I should say
Archie booked it for me. I needed Trinity gone so Fern and Dee
Dee could get Hope ready. The plan is when Trinity gets home, I
tell her Fern and Ann took Hope to play with Emma and Charlie
until Wolf's party, and that they would bring her there.

She looks shocked at first, then smiles at me before she
starts to cry. Fuck these hormones again. She launches herself at
me, which takes me by surprise. I go back a step as she wraps
herself around me.

"Thank you so much, Cadence. I need this so bad. I didn't
even realize it until now. With everything that's happened with
our Horde family, the holidays, and us getting pregnant again, I
can't take much more. I'm at my wits end, so thank you for
thinking of me. I plan to enjoy every second of this today."

"I know, babe. Go get ready, and I'll take care of Hope.
Right, little girl? Daddy can handle you this afternoon. We'll
have fun playing with your toys and the cats too."

Trinity smiles before she takes off to get ready for her spa
day.

"Well, we got that part done, didn't we Hope? Let's pray
our other plans fall into place just as easily."

Trinity

Sitting with my feet in the massage bath, I listen to Willow,
Archie, and Dee Dee go on about some rumor they heard. I try to
keep up, but I'm so relaxed, I feel myself falling asleep.

"Trinity, wake up. We need your opinion on this."

I look at Archie, but they're all staring at me.

"What's up? Sorry, Hope's teething and keeping me up at night, not to mention this one giving me indigestion all the time."

"One of the girls that comes to help Ann told her a story about a couple that were engaged, but not married. The girl is ready, but as guys do, he's taking his time. Or so his girlfriend thought. Turns out he had pulled all their family and friends into a surprise wedding. He really listened, and planned the wedding of her dreams. Ann said the girl was pissed because she didn't get to do anything, so we were just saying we wouldn't be mad. In fact, it would be awesome not having to do all that work. What do you think?"

They're all watching me intently. I think about it for a minute or two, then give her my answer.

"I think it would be wonderful to have a man love you so much that he would go to all that trouble to plan a wedding dreams are made of for his girlfriend. Not many guys would do that. Besides, most guys don't know the first thing a girl wants at her wedding. I mean, if I asked Cadence, he would probably give me that sexy grin and be like 'Babe, whatever ya want, I'll get for ya. But fuck, how am I supposed to know what ya like? I'm not a chick, I have a dick.' Then again, he did get me this awesome spa package, so I gotta give him that."

Giggling, I take a sip of my lemon water and look back at the girls, who are all looking at each other funny. Smiles break out on all their faces, and then they turn those smiles on me.

"What? Did I say something funny?"

Dee Dee looks me in the eyes with a glimmer in her own. "Nothing you said was funny, Trinity. You just made us realize how good you are for Cadence, that's all. You have really brought out the best in him."

At this, we all start to giggle like schoolgirls, and proceed to enjoy our much-needed day of beauty.

Chapter 18

Cadence

Hope's Wedding Day Too

I'm sitting on the couch with my head in my hands, listening to my baby girl screaming her little head off, having no idea what the fuck to do. Hearing a knock at the door, I get up and thank God, Fern is finally here.

"Oh my Gosh, Cadence. What's going on?"

"Well, as you can hear, Hope is having her first temper tantrum, and I have no idea how to calm her down. I gave her a bath, washed her hair, and powdered her up just like you said. Then she wanted to get dressed, but I didn't want to fight with her, so I tried to put on that thing? You know. After a bath it looks like an animal. Anyways, she had a fit and hasn't stopped since. It's been like this for ten minutes. Can you please help me? I'm about to pull my hair out."

As Gabriel comes through the door with a canvas bag and a garment bag over his arm, he looks down the hall questioningly at me. Fern walks to him, takes the bags, then comes back to kiss me on the cheek.

"No worries, Cadence. She'll be fine. This is just the first of many, I can guarantee that, so be prepared."

With that, she turns and walks to Hope's room, closing the door behind her. In less than two minutes, I hear Hope stop crying, and to my surprise, I hear her giggling along with Fern. Thank God.

I turn to Gabriel, who's looking at me with a shit-eating grin on his face.

"What are you fucking smiling at, huh? All that was from a tiny little female. I'm screwed, aren't I, Doc?"

He nods before walking over to the fridge. "Want a beer while we wait for the little princess to get ready?"

He grabs two, passes one to me, and we go sit on the couch. Turning my way, he takes a drag off his beer, then reaches over to give my shoulder a squeeze.

"Cadence, I'm proud of you. I want you to know that Fern and I are happy as hell that you found Trinity. Then when Hope came, we had no idea how important she would be to both of us, and not just because of the bone marrow transplant. That little girl stole our hearts. And now, after all the hard work you did planning this wedding, you make me so proud of the man you've become. Gotta tell ya, for a while we were worried, but you pulled your crap together and have become a great man. Congratulations, Cadence, on your wedding day."

I feel so much pride at his words. Gabriel has been a father figure to me, and has always supported me, through the good and the bad times. I put both him and Fern through so much crap in the beginning, and all they ever did was love me.

"Thanks, Gabriel, or should I say Dad. Those words mean the world to me, as I want both you and Fern to be proud of me. Without you guys, along with Des, I would be dead. So please know that even though I don't say it enough, I do love you, and I admire you for the man you are. Hard shoes to follow in, but you make me want to be a better man, better Dad, and now a husband, so thank you for that."

He reaches over and gives me a hug, and then we sit and talk about anything and everything. We're just two guys who enjoy each other's company. One mature guy, who has

98

experienced life and the other younger trying to follow in his footsteps, is learning every step of the way.

Hearing footsteps, we both look up to see Fern approaching.

"Can I have your attention please? I want to present Hope Powers. Hope, honey, come on down and show your daddy and Grandpa Gabriel how you look."

Fern comes to stand by the couch, one hand on Gabriel's shoulder, the other on mine. I hear tap, tap, tap, and then I watch as my beautiful daughter comes down the hall with flowers in her hair, pink cheeks and shiny lips. She looks like a cherub. Her white dress is all lace, and her little white shoes have bows on the top. She's carrying a basket of flower petals as she waddles towards us.

"Daddy, Grammie Fern said I look gorgeeeous. Do I?"

Tears fill my eyes as I look at the miracle Trinity and I created. I pull her to me and hug her tight.

"Hope, you look beautiful. I can't believe how grown up you look. Mommy is going to be so surprised. Now, you need to go with Grammie Fern and Grandpa Gabriel. I'll see you at Uncle Wolf's house, okay."

"Okay, daddy. I yove you."

As they pack up everything and leave, I sit back down and let my emotions take over. My life is finally where I've always wanted it to be, whether I knew it or not. Family, friends, and the love of my life, who gave me the other little love of my life.

Even with all the shit in my past, from Roman, the abuse, and me being a total dick to everyone around me, all it took was one girl with blonde hair and blue eyes to pull me from the bowels of hell, and she did it with something I had always run from—love.

Fuck. I sound like a pussy from one of those books Trinity reads on her Kindle all the time. I reach over, grab my beer, and gulp the rest down.

Chapter 19

Cadence

Here Comes the Bride

Waiting on Trinity in our apartment, I'm starting to panic. What happens if she isn't up for the wedding surprise? All the planning and work everyone put in would be for nothing. I feel sick to my stomach, cold and sweaty, even though I've just taken a shower. My suit's at Wolf's, as is Trinity's dress. Thank God for Willow and Fern, as they were able to quiz Trinity with questions about her

dream wedding gown. Even I don't know what it looks like, but the girls said it was bad luck. Whatever.

Hearing the door open, I look up and feel my chest tighten. Holy shit! An angel just walked into our home. Trinity looks like a dream come true. Not only is her hair done, but her make-up is also. She's breathtaking.

"Wow, babe. You look gorgeous. How was your day?"

She puts her purse down and turns to me. "I felt like a princess. They took such good care of us. We all look so amazing that we should be going somewhere fancy, not just to Wolf's. Where's Hope? Is she still down for her nap?"

"Nope. Fern and Ann came over with Charlie and Emma, looking to see if Hope wanted to go with them and play for a while. She jumped at the chance, so she'll meet us at Wolf's."

She looks at her watch, then back at me with a worried look.

"Oh crap! What time do we need to be at Wolf's? I didn't realize how late it was. Give me twenty minutes to change and we can go. Can you start packing the car up with the stuff in the fridge?"

She turns and takes off down the hall before I can reply. Smiling, I grab the stuff out of the fridge and walk it down to the SUV. Putting everything in the back, I go back up and wait for Trinity as I nervously wring my hands.

Finally, she comes down the hallway, and once again, she takes my breath away. She's in a lacy blue wrap dress that makes her eyes pop. It's fitted, showing off her kick-ass figure, even with the small baby bump. Classy all the way.

Getting up and helping her put her wrap on, she giggles.

"Wow, Cadence. Such a gentleman. Thank you, honey."

I lean down and give her a tender kiss, then we head to Wolf's and to our wedding.

Pulling up to Wolf's, I shut off the vehicle and turn to face Trinity.

"Do you trust me?"

She looks at me confused, then nods her head.

"Good. When the girls come out to get you, go with them and do whatever they say, okay?"

"Cadence, what's going on? You have to tell me, because you're freaking me out."

Grabbing her hands, I pull her closer and kiss her deeply. Once I break the kiss, I look into her eyes. "Trinity, will you marry me?"

She giggles as she raises her hand, wiggling the ring on her finger. "Duh, you asked that already and I said yes. Did you forget?"

"No, but I need you to answer me...please."

"Of course I'll marry you."

I hold her close to me as I whisper in her ear. "Good, 'cause we're getting married tonight."

I wait for it, and it doesn't take her too long to comprehend what I've told her.

"What, are you crazy? How can we get married? There's planning and stuff we have to argue over. How can we do that tonight? What the hell are you talking about?"

I remain quiet until she takes a deep breath. "Everything is waiting on us, Trinity. I wanted to do something special for you, to show you how much you mean to me. Everyone helped, and if you would honor me, all we have to do is walk into Wolf's house and enjoy our wedding. Can you do that for me? I want this more than anything in this world. I want you to be my wife."

Watching her eyes start to get glassy, I grab a tissue from the center console and hand it to her.

"Don't cry, you'll ruin your make-up."

She wipes her eyes, and then looks into mine with a blinding smile. "That's what the girls were talking about. It was you planning the wedding for me. God, I can be so dumb sometimes. Cadence honey. I love you so much. Of course I'll marry you tonight."

At that exact moment, the door opens and the girls walk towards us. I flash the lights once, and I hear Archie yell, "About damn time." They approach us, and open Trinity's door to pull her out. She turns to me and gives me her million-dollar smile before heading off with her posse to get ready for our wedding.

I sit in our SUV, watching them go inside, then the door closes behind them. I just sit there, kind of numb, until Wolf comes out and opens my door.

"Brother, you gonna sit here all night, or do you plan on getting married? Come on, it's all ready for you, and it looks fuckin' out of this world. Yeah, I said it, dude. Let's get you suited up and we can get started."

He pulls me out and I walk into the house, knowing that when I leave tonight, I'll be a married man.

Suddenly, I feel lighter as my happiness takes me over.

Chapter 20

Trinity

Wedding Jitters

Looking in the full-length mirror in Wolf's bedroom, I'm stunned at my reflection. If I ever thought of how I would look on my wedding day, I'm looking at it right now. How did Cadence pull this off without any help from me? Does he really know me that well? Apparently, the answer is yes.

My dress is perfect, and it fits like a glove. Little did I know that Ann is a pretty good seamstress? With just a few nips and tucks, she made an awesome dress perfect. It was simple and elegant with off the shoulder sleeves. Lace is attached to a sweetheart bodice, satin with lace overlay, ending in a mermaid skirt with train. At the waist, a beautiful satin belt with a Swarovski heart crystal sits.

My shoes are white, closed-toe platforms by Nina, with a clutch to match. Underneath, my lingerie is a beautiful powder blue satin and lace. I have the works from the bra, hipster underwear, thigh highs, and a sexy cream lacy garter.

My veil is simple and long, with crystals scattered throughout, ending at the dress train. My hair is done partially up in curls, while the rest lays down my back with crystal pins here and there, thanks to Prudence.

The girls thought of everything from the blue in my undergarments, the diamonds at my neck and ears from Dee Dee as something borrowed, Fern's wedding hanky as something old, and finally, a Swarovski bracelet from Willow and Archie as my something new.

Feeling overwhelmed, I move to sit at the edge of Wolf's bed lost in my thoughts. Never in my wildest dreams would I have thought this possible. Just the brief walk through to get here, Wolf's home has been transformed into the wedding venue of my dreams. Crystals, stars, dangles, doves and so much more than my eyes could take in in the brief time they had. The girls were on a schedule, so they maneuvered me to this room, which had everything waiting.

As they helped me get ready, they were also preparing. All were wearing beautiful deep emerald and lilac shimmery dresses that seemed to change color when they moved. They left it up to me who would be my maid of honor, and I picked Fern, of course. The rest are bridesmaids.

As my mind runs in all directions, I hear a knock at the door before it opens and Wolf walks in. Looking up at him, I realize I've never seen him dressed up. He's wearing a dark grey tuxedo with a deep emerald colored shirt and a lilac tie. His hair is loose around his shoulders, and man, does he look gorgeous and hot.

"Hi, Wolf."

"Hey, Little One. You look stunning. You'll take Cadence's breath away, I guarantee it." He smiles as he comes closer with his hands behind his back, obviously holding something.

As I watch, he hands me a blanket, wrapped with a ribbon. I look up into his eyes and feel the same warm feeling I get every time I'm in his presence. He was always there for me when all the bad stuff in my life came out. He had both Cadence and my backs, and helped us to find each other again. Waiting for him to explain why he's giving me this beautiful looking blanket, I watch many emotions cross his face.

"Trinity, in my culture, we use this blanket in our wedding ceremonies. I want you to have it, and if you decide to use it, I can explain how and when. This one is very special to me." He stops for a moment, struggling with some unknown emotion, then continues on. "I have held on to this for years, and it's time to find it another home. One filled with the love of a newly married couple that are on their joined path together. So please, accept this, Little One, with my heartfelt prayer that you and Cadence only experience the very best in this life you are starting together."

I put the blanket to the side and stand. I put my head to his chest as I wrap my arms around his waist, feeling as always, a peaceful calm whenever I'm around him.

"Wolf, there are no words to express my gratitude for all you have done for me. From the beginning, you have been a constant friend who I have come to depend on. This means the world to me, and I will treasure it. Who's was it, your mothers?"

His arms tighten before he pulls away. As he walks to the door, he turns to me and with a closed expression, he replies. "No, Trinity, it was mine."

Cadence

Why the hell am I a nervous wreck? I'm acting like a bitch, and it's pissing me off. I love Trinity, and I want to marry her, so why all the butterflies and shit? Hearing the door open behind me in Wolf's office, I turn to see Des walking in, closing the door behind him. Not sure what he wants, but I hope there's nothing wrong.

"Hey, kid. How you doin'? You're looking a little nervous, but there's no need to worry. Everyone you wanted here is here, and in about ten minutes, you'll be getting married. I just wanted to let you know how proud I am of you, Cadence."

I nod, then walk over to the couch and sit. He comes and sits beside me, putting his hand on my leg.

"Cadence, take a breath and relax. All the hard work is paying off. It's fuckin' beautiful out there, if I say so myself. Good job. You gonna be okay?"

"Yeah, Des, I am now. Let's get this party started. I'll be out in a minute."

As Des leaves, I take a moment to reflect on the last couple years. Man, did my life take another path once Trinity became a part of it. I thank God every day for bringing her into my life. She doesn't realize it, but she saved me from myself. She and Hope are my life, and that's why I wanted tonight to be perfect.

Time to get married, I guess.

Chapter 21

Trinity

Wedding Ceremony

Everyone's lined up in the house to go out to the gazebo that's set up for the ceremony. It's time, and my mind can't grasp all that was done to get this night together.

I almost lost it when Charlie and Emma walked toward me, holding little Hope's hands, all three of them dressed up. Apparently, Charlie's the ring bearer, Emma's a bridesmaid, and Hope is the flower girl.

Hope looks so perfect in her little dress, with her hair curled around a wreath of flowers on the top of her head, and ribbons falling down her back. Clutched in her hands is a small basket of flower petals. She pulls away from the kids, dropping the basket on the floor, and runs into me arms. As I grab her up, the smile on her face is heartwarming.

"Momma, we're getting married today. How do I look? Am I bootiful?"

I laugh, trying to keep my tears at bay, and I kiss her chubby little cheek.

"Yes, we're getting married, and you look beautiful, honey. Momma loves you, my precious girl."

I love you too, Momma. I wanna get down now."

Setting her feet on the floor, she walks back to Charlie and Emma and picks up her basket before they skip away.

Both Willow and Archie are at my side, making sure there's nothing I need. Archie's making sure I stay hydrated, whereas Willow is my quiet strength. Her presence is like Wolf's, which makes me calmer and able to deal with the shock of everything.

As the line starts to move, I feel my stomach pitch. Knowing with my entire heart that I want to marry Cadence, I start to think it's just nerves, but also a little fear of the unknown. I have no idea what's going to happen next.

Willow says, "Relax, Trin, and breathe. There's nothing to be worried about. I need you to take a deep breath, and enjoy each and every moment of this."

Grabbing their hands in mine, I tell them, "You both are an absolute blessing in my life. I love you girls so much."

Both squeeze my hands back, and then hug me tightly, letting me know they feel the same.

As it comes to their turns to head out, I'm left with Fern. She has been a constant in my new life, like the mother I never had. She turns to me, eyes shining.

"Trinity, you are like my daughter, and I love you so very much. I want you to remember that you and Cadence love each other. Remember to be kind when he is unkind. Be patient when he has lost all patience, and give more than fifty percent, because it is never fifty-fifty. One will always give more than the other. Never go to bed angry because you never know what the next day will bring. Just love each other and your children, and you will have all the blessings you need. I love you, beautiful girl."

I grab her close, as we both fight against our tears. I try to think of something eloquent to say back to her, but once again, I'm at a loss for words, so I give her what I have.

"I love you, Fern. Thanks for being you and loving me the way you do. Love you, Mom."

Daisy clears her throat and gives us the look.

110

"Fern, you're up. I'll straighten Trinity's dress as she heads in."

Fern lets me go, reaching for a hanky in her sleeve and dabs at her eyes with it before she turns and walks out the sliding doors to the waiting ceremony.

Standing there with Daisy, I realize something's bothering her. She keeps pulling on the sleeves of her pretty dress, obviously in discomfort.

"Honey, what's wrong? Are the sleeves bothering you? Let me see."

As I go to reach for the sheer sleeves, she tries to move back, but I get a grip on her arm before she can pull away. When I lift it, I see bruises. Holy crap.

"Daisy, where did you get these bruises on your arm? Holy hell, they look fresh. Please talk to me."

Just as she opens her mouth, I hear the music change. Gabriel approaches with a huge smile on his face and his arm out, ready for me to take it. Looking back, I watch Daisy's face shut down.

"Go on, Trinity, you're up. We'll talk later…go on. Oh, and happy wedding day."

She finishes with a small smile, then bends to straighten my train as I walk to Gabriel, who kisses my forehead and we start to walk out the door.

Cadence

With Wolf at my side, I try to wait patiently as everyone walks down the aisle. First come the bridesmaids to their groomsmen. Then Charlie, Emma and Hope. I almost lose it as my little Hope carefully tosses the petals on the runner. As Charlie starts to speed up, and her adorable little girl voice can be heard over the music.

"Charrrlie, slow down. My job is to throw the petals."

Smiling as everyone laughs, we watch the three make their way down the aisle. Then Fern comes down, looking breathtaking in an emerald green dress, accentuated with faint accents of lilac, which is a little different than the other girls. Now I'm waiting on Gabriel to bring Trinity down the aisle to me. I'm sweating. Feeling a hand on my shoulder, I look to see Wolf grinning.

"Brother, calm down before you pass out or scare everyone away with that look on your face. It's done, Cadence. This is the time to enjoy your hard work. Telling you man, you did good. Just breathe."

As he continues, we hear the music change, and as I'm looking at Wolf, he turns his head and his eyes widen.

"Cadence, your woman is coming now. Look down the aisle at the angel walking towards you."

Scared to look, but knowing I have to, my eyes move from his to the aisle. All the air leaves my lungs and my eyes bug out. Holy shit. Trinity looks just like Wolf said, an angel. Arm in arm with Gabriel, they look like they're floating down the runner. As Gabriel leans down to kiss her cheek, he moves her hand from his arm and gives it to me, then he shakes mine. As soon as we connect, I feel an instant calm take over. As we move to stand next to each other, my heartbeat seems to relax, and my next breath seems to come easier.

Facing the preacher as we hold hands, we start the beginning of the rest of our lives together. We start with the exchange of vows to love, honor and cherish. Then from the pillow Charlie holds, we each give the other a ring. As we listen to the words of how we need to take our marriage vows seriously, all I can feel is Trinity's hand in mine, her shining eyes looking at me. I feel for the first time in my life, I've finally found where I truly belong.

We are in the gazebo under a sky filled with stars. The gazebo is lit up with twinkling star lights and ribbons, blowing in the gentle wind. With the evening temperature dropping, Wolf turned on the heaters, which took away the chill, making the evening surreal and serene.

Finally, I hear the words I've been waiting for.

"Cadence, you may kiss your bride."

I reach for Trinity and pull her close, pressing my lips to hers. It's our first kiss as a married couple, and it feels perfect.

"Ladies and Gentlemen, it is my honor to introduce to you, Mr. & Mrs. Cadence and Trinity Powers.

As we turn to our family and friends, who are on their feet applauding and cheering, Trinity and I, hand in hand, along with Hope in my arms, walk between them all with the biggest smiles on our faces.

Chapter 22

Trinity & Cadence

Reception

As the caterers are getting everything together outside in the pole barn, the guests are enjoying cocktails and hors d'oeuvres in Wolf's great room and also out on his wrap around deck out front. Looking around, everyone seems to be having a great time.

Looking up at Cadence, I reach for his cheek to get his attention.

"Cadence, this is perfect. I will never forget our wedding day, or that you did all of this for me. I'm speechless, honey. You own my heart."

As he pulls me close and gives me a light kiss, I hear the cheers behind us. Knowing that we have the support and love of our family and friends makes this night even more precious. Feeling a bit warm, I pull away from my husband. I can't help but smile when I think that he is indeed my husband. I tell him I need some air, so we head to the front deck. As people see us coming out, we're surrounded by well wishers. I begin to feel lightheaded, and I realize that I haven't eaten since the spa this afternoon. Immediately, Cadence senses something's off.

"Darlin', what's wrong?"

"Just a bit lightheaded. I haven't eaten since early this afternoon."

I haven't even finished my sentence when Archie comes out the door with a G2 drink and some appetizers on a fancy plate.

"There you are. I was looking all over for you. Here, eat and drink this. Dinner isn't for a while, and I figured you might need something to tide you over."

Cadence laughs at the look on my face as he turns to Archie with a smile.

"Perfect timing. She was just telling me she's light headed from not eating since earlier in the afternoon. Thanks, Archie, for watching out for her."

Archie looks at Cadence in shock. These two argue like brother and sister, rarely having anything nice to say to each other. And for once, instead of it being the two of them at each other, Archie turns, and in her usual Archie fashion, she yells to some guests, "Out of those chairs! The bride and groom need to sit for a bit."

The two guests immediately get up and go in the house as Archie brushes them off, then helps me sit with the dress and all.

"Once you eat and feel better, we'll bustle the train for you. Willow and Prudence were shown how to do it at the dress shop."

With that, she turns and leaves us to our small corner with the stars above us as we nibble on some fantastic snacks and G2.

As we relax on the deck, talking quietly to ourselves, I see Jagger and his girlfriend Sabrina coming from his car. Watching them, something about her doesn't sit well with me, so I turn to Cadence before they get to the house.

"Do you like that girl with Jagger?"

"Don't know her, but I know he's into her. Des said he's going through condoms like there's no tomorrow."

I elbow him in the ribs.

"Cadence, they're just kids."

As we're talking, Daisy comes out the front door, heading our way with a hesitant smile on her face.

"Trinity, Cadence. I wanted to wish you both all the best. Congratulations, your wedding was beautiful."

As she's speaking, Jagger and Sabrina make their way to us. When Daisy spots Sabrina, her whole demeanor changes. When Jagger reaches around Daisy to give me a kiss, I can't believe what I see. This little Sabrina wench grabs Daisy on the under part of her arm where the bruises are. Pain instantly shows on Daisy's face, and I watch Sabrina smirk, until her eyes meet mine. Immediately, she has that innocent look on her face, reaching to grab Jagger's hand. I'm shocked at what I've just witnessed, and as I'm trying to comprehend it, Daisy turns and goes back inside. Once the kids give us their congrats, they head in. Cadence turns to me, anger taking over his features.

"What the fuck was that? Did that bitch just fuck with Daisy right in front of us? 'Cause that's what I thought I saw."

"Cadence, calm down. From the way Daisy took off, she doesn't want any drama. But yes, that's what I saw too. We're gonna have to tell Dee Dee and Des."

Before he can reply, the door swings open and Fern leans out.

"Come on, kids. Everything's ready. You need to make an entrance at your reception."

We both look at each other, knowing something evil and wrong is going on, and we need to put an end to it. The question is when do we do it? Daisy's keeping it to herself for a reason, and I don't want to make things worse for her. We'll have to wait and not say anything tonight.

Chapter 23

Trinity

Reception

Walking hand in hand with Cadence, the pole barn looks like a fantasy come to life.

The walls have been covered with a shimmery material that changes colors when the lights hit it. There are swags of material with lights hanging in front of the ceiling, giving the room a soft dreamy look. Round and square tables are covered in creamy tablecloths with shimmery sheer runners. Centerpieces include candles of different shapes and sizes, with a simple small vase of orchids in a violet color. It's stunning.

The center of the barn has a dance floor with lights gently flowing around the pole barn.

A buffet is set up to one side, while the other has a bar and bartender. How the heck did they get this set up so fast? It was what, ninety minutes ago that we got married? I knew the food was in Wolf's state-of-the-art kitchen, and now all of it is set up on warmers to keep it hot.

We walk through to the head table that holds our wedding party. In the center are two empty chairs, and next to one is Hope, sitting in a highchair decorated with bows. She sees us and starts to wave her hands excitedly at us. Reaching her, I bend and give her a kiss, and so does Cadence. Once we're seated, the DJ brings the mic to us. Cadence stands, reaching for it and clearing his throat.

"Trinity, Hope, and I want to thank you for being here to celebrate our wedding. It means a lot to us, so make sure to eat, drink and party."

Everyone claps as he sits back down. As soon as he does, Fern comes up to the table, telling us to go get some food. Thank goodness the girls bustled the dress, or I'd be dragging everywhere. They also took off the long veil, leaving me with a small shoulder length one.

As everyone gets food and begins to eat, a photographer starts to take pictures, which Cadence explains to me that he wants real shots, not posed. It would be great to hang them on our walls.

The food is delicious, and as I eat and feed Hope, every once in a while, we can hear the clinking of the glasses. As was tradition each time, Cadence smiles giving the thumbs up to the guests and gives me a deep, wet kiss. He also reaches over and gives Hope her own little kiss. She is eating it up the little ham.

When dinner starts to wind down, the DJ once again appears with the mic. This time, he hands it to Fern, who stands nervously holding index cards in her hands.

"Hello, everyone. I'm Fern, the Matron of Honor. I am kind of like a second Mom to both Trinity and Cadence. When I met Trinity, I knew that she was the one for him. She was beautiful, as you can see, but also kind and shy. She was quiet, but when she let loose, she was funny and spunky. As they moved through their relationship, all I had to do was look at the way Trinity looked at Cadence to know how much she loved him. I don't have enough time to share everything she did for me, but I will say that she's a miracle. Cadence came to us in the same kind of way. Took some time, but his true being came out, and I fell in love with the young man. Together, they are beginning their family with Hope, and we all know another one is on the way. To Trinity and Cadence. May all their wishes come true.

So please raise your glasses. To life, love, and a much deserved happily ever after."

Reaching over, both Cadence and I hug Fern. She then turns and hands the mic to Wolf as he stands.

"I would like to start off with an Apache Blessing poem."

Now you will feel no rain,

for each of you will be shelter for the other.

Now you will feel no cold,

for each of you will be warmth to the other.

Now there will be no loneliness,

for each of you will be companion to the other.

Now you are two persons,

but there is only one life before you.

May beauty surround you both in the

journey ahead and through all the years,

May happiness be your companion and

your days together be good and long upon the earth.

"Remember these words, Trinity and Cadence, as you start your married life. I wish you a life filled with joy, hope in your soul, and love in your hearts. Everyone raise your glasses to Trinity and Cadence. May Mother Earth provide you with everything you will need to live a life full of love. Congratulations to Little One, and my Brother."

Wiping the tears from my eyes, I stand, falling into Wolf's arms. Hugging him tight, I feel Cadence beside me, his arm around Wolf, hugging both of us. The poem was so beautiful, I want to frame it and put it up so we can have it forever.

Once the toasts are done, we cut the beautiful cake with Hope's help. She even got to put a tiny piece in both Mommy and Daddy's mouths. Then the light dims, and the DJ calls us out for our first song of the night. Curious to see what Cadence has picked, my heart stops when I hear the first few notes of *Unchained Melody* by the Righteous Brothers. My God, how did he remember this is the song we danced to on that first date, after we got back together? Feeling so many emotions, we sway on the dance floor, hands wrapped around each other. As the song comes to an end, the DJ's voice comes over the speakers.

"Cadence had a hard time with picking the first song, so that was the first song Trinity and he danced to during their first official date. This is the other song that Cadence states says it all."

I hear Ella James' *At Last*, and I feel the tears fill my eyes and start to run down my cheeks. I look up at Cadence, and he leans down to kiss me, then moves to my ear to whisper, "Trinity, at last, I have found my Love. You, babe, are it. You can't get rid of me now."

Pulling my body closer to his, I feel his heart beating under my ear. His hand lightly caresses my lower back, while his other hand stays at my neck, keeping me close. The words from the song are etched on my heart as I realize that yes, I have found my love too, and his name is Cadence Powers.

Chapter 24

Fern & Gabriel

Welcoming the New Year In

Fern

Watching as the time draws closer to midnight, the kids are struggling to stay awake as the reception is in full swing. The dance floor is packed with everyone, young and old. The DJ is a master mixer as he plays every type of music from the Jitterbug, the Twist, Electric Slide, to dance and party music for the younger crowd. Gabriel and I are taking a much-needed break from the dancing with Charlie and Emma. Sitting at a table, sipping my wine, I look to Gabriel, who is watching the kids fly all over the dance floor, a happy smile on his face. Reaching for his hand, I bring it to my heart.

"Having a good time, honey? Wasn't it a beautiful wedding? Both Trinity and Cadence look so much in love. What a blessed day. I'm so happy for them, aren't you?"

"Sugar, I couldn't be happier. Having you at my side, those two youngin's running amuck, and Cadence and Trinity settled, it's the third best day of my life."

"What was your first, Gabriel?"

"Surprised you would have to ask. Definitely best day of my life is the day you married me. The second best day was when we were told you were in remission. Two days I will never forget as long as I live."

Dang it all. I feel the tears in my eyes again. How he does it, I don't know, but I do know that my Gabriel is a once in a lifetime guy.

"I love you, Gabriel."

"Treasure that, Sugar. Love you too."

Dee Dee & Des

Dee Dee

Feeling the day getting the best of me, I lean into Des as his arms come around me, pulling me close.

"Dee Dee, you outdid yourself. This was an amazing wedding. Can't believe you pulled it off on such short notice. Might be in the wrong business, babe."

I giggle at his words because I've been thinking the same thing. I enjoyed all the planning, and had so much fun, but to start my own business is a huge undertaking. Putting my hands over his, I squeeze.

"Funny you should say that. I'm considering doing this as a career, but I've got to be honest. I'm scared, and I don't want to leave Wheels & Hogs. Maybe we can talk about it later, and weigh the pros and cons. You know how much work is involved with start-up businesses, and to say I don't have a ton of available money is definitely a problem. Thanks, though, for your kind words honey. I'm glad you had a good time. I think everyone did, and if they didn't? That's their problem. Still have the fireworks at midnight, so that should be a blast, no pun intended."

Des laughs. I love his laugh—deep, rough, and from the gut.

Wolf & Axe

Wolf

As we're setting up the fireworks with the guys from Tranquility Fire Department, Axe leans in close.

"How you doin', Brother? Can't be easy, the wedding and all."

"I'm fine, Axe. It was a long time ago, and I can't change anything, so just be happy for Cadence and Trinity."

"I get ya, Bro, but be honest. Have you thought about Star with all this going on? I have, and dude, I wasn't married to her."

"To be honest, I have thought about her. How could I not? What happened was out of my control, and even after all these years, nothing has ever turned up. I have no idea if she's dead or alive."

"Maybe it's time for you to move on."

"Yeah, been thinkin' on that too. Something happened over Christmas, I'm sure you heard. Willow and I kissed under the mistletoe, and I can't stop thinking about it."

Axe grins at me, his eyes sparkling.

"Well it's about damn time. She's been crushing on you forever. Move on, Wolf, and don't wait too long. The past is the past. I know Prudence told you what she saw at the Master's compound, but even that's not proof Star is still alive."

As we finish up the preparations, my mind weighs Axe's words. Is it time for me to move on? The thought scares me, but it's something to ponder in the upcoming months, I guess.

Daisy, Jagger & Sabrina

Daisy

Coming out of the bathroom, I'm not paying attention when I feel my hair being pulled from behind. As I start to scream in pain, I hear her voice.

"Don't even think about screaming, you little bitch. Better figure out a way to make Cadence and Trinity believe they didn't see what they saw."

When she releases my hair, I fly forward, right into Jagger's body.

"What the hell, Daisy? You sneaking some of the alcoholic drinks Sis?"

Looking into my brother's eyes, he immediately sees the pain before I can hide it. He looks behind me and sees Sabrina standing there, then suddenly his eyes change, and I immediately become frightened. Not for me, but for her.

"What did you just do, Sabrina? Have you been fuckin' with my sister all this time?"

She moves towards him as he holds me tightly to him, my face smashed into his chest. Raising his hand, she stops.

"Don't. I've had a feeling that something's been going on, and now I know. Every time I find you two together, my sister is either tripping, getting up from falling, or looking like she's in pain. I get it now bitch. We're done. You don't fuck with my family."

I gasp at his words. I turn to see Sabrina's face in shock before she unleashes her shit.

126

"Wait, did I hear you right? You are breaking up with me because of your little dorky sister? Are you serious? Whatever, dude. I was getting bored with you anyways. You're worse than a dog in the sack. It's your loss, Jagger, not mine. I'll call one of my girls to pick me up. Oh, and Daisy, I'll see you in school. Just letting you know."

With that, she turns and leaves, phone to her ear.

"Shortcake, why didn't you tell me? I would have taken care of it way before tonight. What the hell has been going on?"

Looking up into his concerned face, I realize this is just going to make it worse.

"Jagger, I know you mean well, but this is going to make my life a living hell, or I should say *more* of a living hell. You have no idea."

Cadence & Trinity

Trinity

Being held against Cadence is the perfect place to be. Feeling his tight muscles against me feels phenomenal. Hope's in his other arm, fighting sleep, so she can see the stars burst in the sky. Her words.

"Babe, you happy?"

"Yes. I've never been this happy. It's actually a little scary because I'm waiting for the dream to end and the nightmare to begin again. Don't mean to be such a downer, but you know what I mean."

He nods, shifting Hope to his hip as he pulls me even closer.

"Baby, I totally get it, but tonight starts our dreams. No more nightmares. We've both had enough? Enjoy this night because tomorrow, we're off for our honeymoon. Fern and Gabriel are taking Hope, and we have 4 nights, 3 days to ourselves. Aren't you curious about where we're going?"

"I'm so excited, and since the girls packed my bags, I guess I can wait for the surprise. I am loving this so much."

Smiling down at me, he kisses my forehead.

"Anything for you, babe. It's going to be awesome, just you and me. It might be a bit remote and simple, but I think you'll enjoy it."

"Now you have my interest piqued. Where are we going?"

"We're going to Galena. I have a cabin in Eagle Ridge. Remember we were on the computer, looking for places we want to go? You saw it and put it on your wish list. Well, we're going, and the pictures are gorgeous, Trin. The clubhouse has all kinds of stuff and buffets, but I figure we'll be too busy to leave the cabin much."

He winks, and I get his meaning, bringing a blush to my cheeks. But I love the idea of Cadence and me in a cabin, alone.

Wolf & Willow
Welcoming 2016

As we all listen to the countdown from the DJ, everyone's waiting for that magical number. As we wait for 2016 to enter, I look around until I find Willow's eyes on me. As the numbers get closer to one, and everyone's holding onto their sweethearts, I make up my mind. As I walk towards her, Archie and

Prudence actually give her a small shove. Just as the DJ announces 2016 is here, I reach for Willow kiss her

"Happy New Year, Willow. I'm feeling 2016 is going to be good to the both of us, *Hopa*."

I press my lips to hers again. When I feel her tongue touch my lips, I lose it. Grabbing her, my tongue pushes its way in to tangle with hers, as we kiss hard and deep.

Yeah, this will be worth it.

Axe, Ugly, Bear, Des

Axe

As we all watch my brother holding Willow in his arms, kissing the shit out of her, I look to the guys around me with a huge grin on my face.

"It's about fuckin' time he gets his shit together. That girl has had it bad for him for as long as I've known her."

Des nods. "Axe, just saying'. Your brother hurts Willow, he'll answer to me."

I nod as both Ugly and Bear second his words.

Looking back, first to Willow, then Wolf, then Jagger with his arm around Daisy, who looks like some serious shit just went down, I think to myself—2016 is gonna be interesting for sure.

From the Author

Thank you for your continued support of the Horde in my Wheels & Hogs series. If you enjoyed this book please take the time to leave a short honest review on Amazon, B&N, iTunes and Goodreads. Each review counts and it is like telling other readers how much you enjoyed this book.

Amazon assists authors with marketing of their books by the number of reviews they have received.

A humble thank you for your honest review.

Stalking Links

Facebook (Like) http://bit.ly/dmearl14
Facebook (Readers Group)
https://www.facebook.com/groups/DMsHorde/

Amazon http://bit.ly/amazondmearl
Twitter http://bit.ly/twitterdmearl
Goodreads http://bit.ly/goodreadsdmearl
Pinterest https://www.pinterest.com/dauthor/
YouTube http://bit.ly/DMEarlYouTube
Newsletter Sign-Up http://bit.ly/newsletterdmearl
Website https:// dmearl.com/

WHEELS & HOGS Series

<u>Connelly's Horde</u>

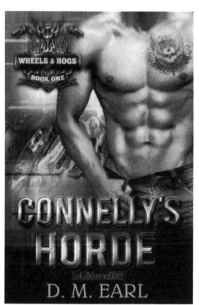

Welcome to Desmond Connelly's Horde or better known as his extended family at Wheels & Hogs Garage. For years these survivors have been dealing with what life throws them while trying to move forward from the atrocities in their lives. Some have secrets not shared while others are working through problems that are continually present in their lives.

Follow Des as he introduces you to each one of his crew at Wheels & Hogs in this short Novella. Start to understand how a group of strangers become not only friends but family over the years. Get a snapshot of why when life pushes you down, in this garage, you push back until you are on your feet again.

Cadence Reflection

Cadence Powers is tattooed, pierced, and panty dropping gorgeous. Women love him and men want to be him. It appears to the world that he has it all, but what people don't see is that Cadence is a damaged haunted man, held back by untold secrets that keep him from living a real life.

When he meets Trinity Vinkers, he feels as if he can finally live the life he desperately wants. However, just as their friendship begins to grow, one stupid act causes that friendship to shatter, all because he lets his guard down allowing her into his life.

Trinity appears to be the light to Cadence's dark. Innocent, naïve, and goofy, she seems to bring out the best in everyone around her, but she has her own dark secret. Her persona allows her to fake her way through life, at least until she meets him. Trying not to let her feelings for Cadence get the best of her is taken out of her hands when she makes a wrong decision that leaves her left with an unexpected fallout.

As life takes both Cadence and Trinity down a path that neither will forget, they are unaware of the evil lurking around them. It's watching, waiting to step in and take everything from Cadence.

As the young lovers struggle with their secrets, a close friend will also be fighting for something,... her life. As time goes by, Cadence and the Horde from Wheels & Hogs decide that they have to do whatever it takes to keep what is theirs safe, even as death hovers around like a dark angel.

Gabriel's Treasure

Gabriel "Doc" Murphy found the woman he'd planned to treasure for the rest of his life in a young, shy girl he had seen being bullied in a hallway between classes whey they were just kids. Over the years, Doc loved and protected her with all he had, until the day came when he received news that there was something that could take her away from him… Cancer. Being faced with the possibility of losing the love of his life, Doc would turn the world inside-out to save and keep the only love that could shatter him, body and soul, if he couldn't save her.

Fern knew the instant she fell into Gabriel's arms all those years ago, that she had found her "one and only." He became her everything—owning her heart and soul. As they made it through their life journey together, nothing could tear their unbreakable bond. Life struggles, financial losses, and even devastating miscarriages didn't stand a chance until the day she received the phone call that finally shattered their world to the core, leaving Fern preparing for the fight of her life.

As Doc and Fern struggle through each day, praying for a miracle, one presents itself. Do they dare have hope, or do they accept that the fight is over as a dark shadow waits patiently to make a move to alter their lives forever.

The Journals Trilogy

Anguish: The Journals Trilogy #1

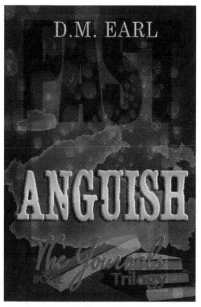

My name is Quinn and in one night my life changed forever. I lost not only part of my family, but also a huge part of who I was. Struggling to make it through each dark day, uncertain of everything in my life, I'm barely living just existing until a professional suggests I start writing down my thoughts in a journal.

My journals help me muddle through the personal and emotional baggage. Allow me to manage the past with all my Anguish; to function in the present plotting Vengeance; and to hope for my Awakening to a future full of all my dreams for a better life.

That is, until my past comes full force into my present and threatens my future. And the only person who can help me is someone from my past. The same person who has been around in the shadows protecting me, even when I didn't know he was there, apparently has always had my back.

Vengeance: The Journals Trilogy #2

I am a survivor.

Ten years ago, my world was shattered. One night changed my life forever by a sadist who took everything from me, just because he could. And while he did this, a green-eyed stranger watched and did nothing … or so I thought.

When my past and present collide, I am swept away by all the memories, horrors, and dreams of my past.

I want revenge.

And finally, after all the years of pain and sacrifices I've had to make, an opportunity presents itself. Within a twenty-four hour period, my tormenter and my green-eyed watcher enter my life once again.

Seeing this as my chance, I begin to make use of my blue journal, detailing my plans for revenge; taking matters into my own hands. Will I have what it takes to ignore what is right and wrong? To bring myself to make the men still alive pay for what they took from me? And how do I forgive the man I hold partially responsible when he's the one supplying me with the means to get what I want?

With only a small window of time available, I have to be ready to take back my life, consequences be damned.

Because of my ANGUISHED past, my present will always be filled with VENGEANCE.

I am Quinn. This is my life—my story.

See Also

The Portland, ME, novels by author Freya Barker.

Web: http://www.freyabarker.com

"From Dust" (Portland, ME, #1)
August, 2015

Pain punished her....

The bottle numbed her....

Guilt kept her trapped....

In the dark alley of a pub, the words "Please don't" take hold of her heart and break the silence she seeks. Thinking herself beyond redemption, she tentatively grabs on to the slim thread of hope that unfolds inside of her.

He never expected the shadow of a woman he finds on the floor of his washroom to bring him the air—the balance and the light he's been missing.

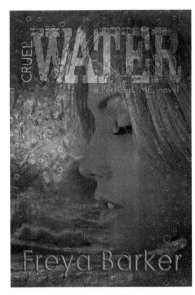

"Cruel Water" (Portland, ME, #2) March, 2016

Innocence marked her…

Violation crippled her…

Love left her raw…

The life she carefully rebuilt is challenged when she is confronted with the sins from her past. The carefully applied protection is at once ripped away, leaving her exposed and vulnerable.

Her single night of indulgence with the silver-eyed stranger is only the beginning. He sees right to the heart of her and she is unable to ward off emotions that have been deeply buried. With the sting of betrayal still fresh in her soul, she's surprised to find herself opening up to the honest integrity of the sharp-eyed, rough-looking biker.

When he lost everyone who mattered, he was left without roots and learned to be content simply living in the moment. Completely unprepared for the feisty blonde bartender with old pain marring her clear-blue eyes, he questions his own rules of detachment, as she unwittingly finds a way under his skin.

Appearances deceive and when the masks fall away, revealing deep, dark secrets, there is nothing left but to hang onto each other and survive the storm

62268222R00079

Made in the USA
Lexington, KY
02 April 2017